"I did not paw you. In fact, I did nothing to warrant being half drowned with the dirty, soapy contents of that bucket. But since you seem to have pronounced me guilty, well then, I think the crime should fit the punishment." So saying, he snatched her off the stool and into his arms and had planted an angry kiss upon her lips before she had sufficient time to jerk them away.

The bucket dropped with a clang. The maid's fingernails targeted his lordship's cheek but were intercepted by a quick, firm clasp of her wrist. Her rather small but quite stout boot contacted his trousered shin, but the kiss went on.

An imperious command barked from the doorway. "Release her at once!"

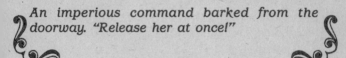

Also by Marian Devon
Published by Fawcett Books:

AN UNCIVIL SERVANT

Marian Devon

FAWCETT CREST • NEW YORK

A Fawcett Crest Book
Published by Ballantine Books
Copyright © 1993 by Marian Pope Rettke

Library of Congress Catalog Card Number: 93-90538

ISBN 0-449-22159-8

Manufactured in the United States of America

First Edition: January 1994

Prologue

ANY ACQUAINTANCE OF LADY LAVINIA PICKERING'S who happened to visit the British Museum on a certain February morning in 1827 might have discovered her there. Her ladyship's attention was not, however, focused upon the spoils of the Egyptian campaign which had drawn her to Great Russell Street. Instead, she was engaged in earnest conversation with a plump, bald-headed, almost elderly little man dressed in tights and gaiters. His eyes sparkled with enthusiasm behind a pair of silver-framed round glasses. He gestured fulsomely and often. He appeared to be expounding upon some favorite theme.

A prudent person, spying the familiar fanatical expression beginning to form upon Lady Lavinia's countenance, might have been well advised to slip quietly out of the great hall, unobserved.

Chapter
One

MRS. ABINGDON, A PLUMP, ATTRACTIVE, MODISHLY dressed lady of middle years, stood at her parlor window and watched her friend hurry up Wimpole Street. It was obvious that Mrs. Oliver was agitated.

Her straw-colored pelisse, of the very latest fashion with an elongated waistline and a bell-shaped skirt, fairly swooshed as she hurried along. The strings of her matching wide-brimmed hat dangled untied. Her pale blue kid gloves were tightly crumpled in one hand.

Her friend's state did not come as a shattering surprise to Jane Abingdon. Adelaide was almost always agitated. Even so, Jane braced herself. The soothing noises were already upon her lips when Addie burst into the room, exclaiming, "She's up to another one of her starts, I know she is!" She was

2

waving a note in the air—the duplicate, Jane had no doubt, of the one she herself had just received.

She coaxed her friend to a seat on the sofa facing a June-idle fireplace while she retrieved her own message from the worktable, where she'd left it. "Let's see yours," she said as she came to sit beside Addie.

The messages were identical. *Come at once. Have a marvelous scheme in mind.*

"Thank goodness you got one, too."

Addie's face did not reflect the relief her words implied. "Misery loves company" might have been a better comment.

Of the three friends who had been bosom bows since their nursery days, two were now widows, the other had never married. Addie, as she was fond of pointing out, was the youngest of the trio, not having yet reached her fiftieth birthday, while the other two had passed that ominous milestone a few months previously. She was a small, thin woman, "skinny," the uncharitable might even say. Her hair was mousy, the result of an incipient invasion of gray upon light brown. Large, ingenuous blue eyes were the best feature of a face that might still be termed pretty on those few occasions when it was anxiety-free.

"She's been working up to something for ages. All the signs are there. You're bound to have noticed, Jane. The way she stares off into space without hearing a word that's spoken to her. And those odd books she's been getting from the circulating library. Not proper books at all like *The Bride of Lammermoor* or *Sense and Sensibility*. But ones having to do with strange subjects that no one could possibly wish to read about."

"Such as?" her friend prompted.

"Oh, I don't remember exactly. Peculiar things. Like North American Indians and their customs. And travel books on outlandish places. Fishing. That sort of thing. Not at all the kind of books any conventional English gentlewoman would wish to read."

"But then, Lavinia Pickering is not a conventional English gentlewoman."

"It's all very well for you to make light of this," Addie snapped. "But I know she is up to no good. She has been, well, too quiet now for ages. Oh, it isn't any one thing I can put my finger on. It's just that after all these years I should know when Lavinia is up to something. And so should you."

Jane Abingdon was forced to acknowledge the hit. But she tried to qualify it. "I'll admit that I have had my suspicions. But look on the bright side. Perhaps this latest scheme will not involve us."

"Not involve us!" Addie's voice rose both in pitch and volume. "Don't talk like a sapskull, Jane. Whenever did Lady Lavinia Pickering go off on some madcap escapade without involving us? Surely you have not forgotten the time she decided that fox hunting was cruel and barbaric and should be banned and we were nearly run down by the Quorn?"

"No, I have not." Her friend shuddered at the memory. "But I am trying my best to do so."

"Or the time we marched up and down in front of Buck House, carrying placards that said QUEEN CAROLINE FOREVER? It was no thanks to Lavinia that we did not wind up in the Tower for treason."

"Oh, really now. That's coming it a bit too strong." Still, Jane blanched a bit at the memory.

"Bear in mind," she rallied, "we were younger then. Passing the half-century mark has a way of tempering one's outlook. Even Lavinia is bound to have mellowed."

"Humph!" Addie's snort was eloquent. She waved her note underneath Jane's nose. " 'Come at once!' " she quoted. " 'Have marvelous scheme in mind.' Does that sound mellow? And if you think my cousin can be content with merely flying off into the boughs all by herself, you should think again. Oh, no. Lavinia will be sure to drag us into her escapade."

"Well, just remember there are two of us. This time we shall simply have to remain firm."

Jane tried to reflect that resolution in her tone of voice. But somehow the words rang hollow even to her ears.

Lady Lavinia Pickering's butler had been a footman in her father's household when she and her two friends had spent their summers on the earl's country estate. The young Moffatt had devoted himself to extracting the trio from mischief and had prevented many of their escapades from coming to light. This proprietary interest had not diminished with the years.

When he opened the door of a large, imposing residence on Grosvenor Street to the two ladies, an anxious look marred a countenance more patrician than servant-class. He barely gave them time to greet him and uncharacteristically ignored Mrs. Oliver's polite inquiry as to the state of his health. "Her ladyship is in the library," he announced in stentorian tones, then whispered, "But could I have a brief word with you first, Mrs. Abingdon?"

"Of course." Jane sighed inwardly. "Addie, tell Lavinia I'll be along in a second or two. Tell her I've just stopped to give Moffatt my mother's rheumatism remedy."

"Oh, dear," Addie wailed nervously but softly. She did not wish to beard the lioness in her den alone. "Do hurry," she pleaded over a shoulder as she left the two standing in the entryway of an enormous marble hall.

"Now then, what is it, Moffatt?"

Jane Abingdon was well accustomed to her position in the triumvirate of friends. Whereas Lavinia was the undisputed leader and Addie the baa-lamb of their group, she was generally regarded as the sensible one and was often requested to make her headstrong friend see reason. The fact that since the age of seven Jane had never once succeeded in that noble endeavor had not cooled the hope that springs eternal. Particularly not in Moffatt's ancient breast.

"It's about her ladyship, ma'am." He then unconsciously echoed Addie's words. "I'm afraid she's up to one of her starts again."

"Indeed? And why do you say so?"

"Well, ma'am, for one thing, she has that faraway look she always gets when she's scheming. And for another, she doesn't even hear you when you speak to her. Or, if she does hear and answers, nine times out of ten it has nothing at all to do with what you've just said to her. For instance, yesterday I mentioned that Cook was wondering whether to do the partridges that evening or hold them over for luncheon today, and she replied that, yes, the yellow bedchamber did need airing. Said she'd been noticing a musty smell for some time now."

"Well, at least she stayed on domestic matters."

Jane's attempt at humor earned her a reproachful glance. She switched to a rallying tone. "I'll admit that all the signs are there, Moffatt. But that doesn't mean, necessarily, that she'll go off on some sort of rattle-pated tangent. She's probably simply bored. Perhaps something will happen to distract her. Shouldn't Lord Pickering be coming soon?"

"His lordship has postponed his visit. Again. You know how he hates the Metropolis, Miss Jane." It was a further sign of the butler's agitation that he slipped back forty years in his mode of address.

"Well, that is too bad. But perhaps you're refining too much on her ladyship's moods."

"Begging your pardon, Miss, but I do not think boredom is her ladyship's problem this time. I really think her—'peculiarities'—began when the new upstairs maid arrived."

"Indeed? That's odd. Her ladyship has not mentioned having a new maid."

"Well, I am not surprised that her ladyship did not choose to mention it." Moffatt's face mirrored a long-time disapproval. "You are aware, Miss Jane, how she has always insisted upon hiring the servants herself."

"Yes, I am. But it is certainly no reflection upon you, Moffatt," she said soothingly. "It's just that she insists that people living under the same roof should have a certain—aura, is it?—which she claims to be able to detect immediately."

Moffatt's privileged position as an old retainer allowed him the luxury of a sniff. "I really couldn't say as to their 'aura,' Miss Jane. But heretofore her ladyship has always engaged competent servants."

7

"Oh? And this one can't do the job? Well, I expect that if you speak to her ladyship about it—"

"Begging your pardon, but I *have* spoken. And when I pointed out that the young person is totally inept, all Lady Lavinia would say was 'Oh, she is young. She will learn.'"

"Well, I expect she has a point. I am certain that Mary can teach her everything she needs to know."

"I don't think you quite understand, Miss Jane. It's not a mere matter of incompetence. There is something altogether odd about this young person. For one thing, I don't think she has ever worked a day in her life."

"Oh, really?" It was the butler's somber tone as much as the words he spoke that added to Jane's unease.

"And what's more, I don't believe she had any references at all. But when I asked her ladyship about it, she went all starchy and told me that she had been engaging servants for thirty years and certainly knew the procedure by now. But," he added darkly, "I noticed she never really answered my question.

"And the worst part of the situation is that the new maid does not fit in here. If it weren't too fanciful for words," he sniffed, "I would say that her 'aura' is all wrong. The other girls are uncomfortable with her, you see. Oh, she is pleasant enough. And I will say she tries. But she's—aloof—don't you know. Keeps herself to herself. And of course the other servants noticed right off the way she was dressed when she came here. The fact is, Miss Jane, she was wearing a costume that would have looked more at home in the drawing room than in the servants' hall. When our Mary mentioned her

8

finery, she went all pink and said that a former employer had put on weight and passed along her outgrown things." He sniffed again. "A Banbury tale if I ever heard one. Oh, I don't doubt that the clothes were given to her, all right. But not by any *female*."

Mrs. Abingdon's eyebrows rose. "You surely are not saying . . ."

"What I am saying, Miss Jane, is simply this. We have a new maid who has never done a lick of work in her entire life and has an unholy amount of good looks. I can only suppose she was hired by some husband for the latter quality and then turned out by his wife without a reference."

"But that doesn't explain why Lavinia would hire her. She's not so easily gulled, you know."

"I do know. That is why I'm so uneasy. I do wish you would go take a look at this person before you join the other ladies, Miss Jane. I'd like to know what you make of the situation."

"Very well. But don't expect much. For if there is one godly thing about Lady Lavinia, it is that she, too, moves in mysterious ways. And if there is any connection between hiring a maid unfit to do the job and her present moodiness, it is probably that she was just too abstracted to pay proper attention. But I will go and take a look at the young woman, Moffatt, and then try to bring up the subject tactfully with Lavinia. Now, where will I find this so-called maid?"

"She is supposed to be turning out the yellow bedchamber. Though what a shambles she will make of that doesn't bear thinking on, Miss Jane."

Mrs. Abingdon had already opened the door to the yellow chamber before it occurred to her that she might need a better excuse for doing so than snooping. She was racking her brain to find one, when it dawned upon her that though she had not intended to sneak up on the unwary maid, thanks to well-oiled hinges, she had done so. The young person in mobcap and apron stood motionless with her back toward the door, holding a feather duster aloft in her hand like a regal scepter. And, unless Jane badly mistook the matter, she was crying softly.

"Ahem."

Jane cleared her throat politely and nearly startled the poor girl out of her skin. She whirled toward the door like a cornered animal.

Jane's first glance confirmed two things: the maid had, indeed, been crying, and yes, she did possess more than her fair share of good looks, though Moffatt's term "unholy" hardly seemed to apply. "Angelic" would have been more apt, Jane thought as the young person stared at her through enormous luminous blue eyes. The face was all that Botticelli could have asked for. Flaxen hair curled out from under the mobcap. And the figure was not sufficiently concealed underneath the voluminous apron to ward off a stab of envy in Jane's well-padded breast.

The chambermaid recovered sufficiently to bob a curtsy. And Jane had the uncomfortable feeling that now she was being sized up rather thoroughly. Certainly the gaze bent upon her was more analytical than subservient. She began to feel like the nosy intruder that she was.

"Er—Kitty, is it?"

"Yes, mum." The maid bobbed her curtsy once again.

"I am Mrs. Abingdon, one of Lady Lavinia's oldest friends. I have lost a handkerchief—a very special one that my eldest niece gave me. She'd worked my initials on it, don't you see." Jane found herself babbling under the steady gaze, and, with effort, reined in her tongue. "I thought perhaps," she continued in a more dignified manner, "that I might have left it here the last time I spent the night. Have you happened upon it?"

"Why, no, mum. But I shall be 'appy to give a proper 'unt for it."

"Well then, thank you, Kitty. I should appreciate that."

Jane turned to leave, feeling decidedly awkward. She was aware that she had not fooled the girl with her handkerchief story. Kitty had known precisely why she was there. Just why she should be the one put out of countenance by the encounter was mystifying.

For Moffatt was right. The girl was no housemaid. It was hard to put one's finger on the reason for this conclusion. The young woman's accent had been strictly cockney. She had bobbed her curtsies with proper respect. Still, Jane found herself thinking of Covent Garden and Drury Lane.

Perhaps it was the appraising stare that had weakened the performance. Or perhaps Jane, too, had become sensitive to the "aura" thing. Or perhaps her suspicions had been awakened out of respect for Moffatt's acumen. But for whatever reason, Jane was now firmly convinced that if that young person was really a housemaid, she herself must be the empress of China.

Chapter
Two

"WELL, HERE YOU ARE AT LAST, JANE."
Lady Lavinia Pickering looked up from the map laid out upon the library table and impaled her dear friend with a glare. And no one could glare more effectively than Lady Lavinia. Her black eyes were made for boring holes right through one. Her long, thin face and aristocratic nose added to the imperious effect. The severe style of her still-jet-black hair (according to her nephew, Lady Lavinia did not turn gray herself, she achieved that effect in others) did nothing to diminish it. "The next time I send around a note saying 'Come at once,' Jane, feel free to dawdle all you like. Why not go by way of the draper's for bugle trimming?"

Jane refused to be put out of countenance by her friend's heavy sarcasm. She joined Addie by a Pembroke table near one of the two empty fireplaces in the oak-paneled, shelf-lined room. The table was weighed down by a heavy silver tea service, porcelain cups and saucers, and a variety of cakes. "Sorry to keep you waiting." She accepted the cup of tea that Addie poured and took a soothing sip. "I went looking for a handkerchief I've lost. It just occurred to me I might have left it in one of the bedchambers the last time I slept here."

"Fustian." The scornful black eyes saw right through the handkerchief whisker. "Moffatt has been complaining to you as usual and wants your opinion of my new upstairs maid."

Jane did not bother to blush. She was far too familiar by her friend's perspicacity to be overset by it. "Well, you must admit that the young person does not exactly fit the servant mold," she countered.

"Is there any reason that she should?" The black eyebrows rose. "But I did not ask you here to discuss my domestic arrangements. No, indeed. I have things of far greater moment to talk about." A fanatical gleam now lighted up her jet-black eyes.

"Tell me, Addie"—she shifted her gaze toward her cousin, to that timid soul's unease—"what is the most exciting thing you have done of late?"

"Exciting? Well, I cannot say about 'exciting,' but seeing the pantomime performed was certainly thrilling. Though I must say they sorely miss Mr. Grimaldi."

"Humph! And what about you, Jane?"

Jane deliberated while she took a thoughtful bite of seed cake. She had become wary of the direction that the talk was taking. "I don't know that I particularly care for 'exciting.' "

"I know you do not," her friend snapped. "That is not at issue. No, I retract that. It may well be. But do answer my question, Jane. What is the last thing you have done that smacked—even if ever so slightly—of excitement?"

"Well"— Jane spoke thickly through a mouthful of cake—"being present for my grandson's birth was thrilling—to borrow Addie's term."

"Ha! Exactly!" Lavinia sank back in her wing chair and surveyed the two in silence. There was deep pity in her gaze.

Unabashed, Jane helped herself to another cup of tea. "I assume, in light of the notes you sent us, that there is some point you wish to make?"

"It would appear that you and Adelaide have just made it for me. I asked you to come up with the high points of your recent lives and both of you—*both* of you—came up with examples of occasions when you were completely passive."

"And is that so bad? I need not point out, Lavinia, that in order to achieve grandmother status I was at one time obliged to have played the active role in childbirth. Believe me, I will take passive any day."

Addie's muffled snicker earned her a set-down look from her imperious cousin.

Lavinia sat erect again. "The point I am trying to make is simply this. The three of us are no longer young."

"I'm a year and two months younger than you are, Vinia," Addie retorted.

"We are all quite well aware of that oft-repeated fact. And pray do not call me Vinia.

"But as I was saying, we are rapidly approaching our twilight years. And now, instead of living our lives to the fullest while we still possess the vigor and spirit to do so, we are allowing ourselves to drift aimlessly and purposelessly through a pointless round of social activities: assemblies, loo parties, theater, opera. When did we last *do* anything, I ask you?"

Lavinia's voice trembled with passion. Her eyes glowed with a suppressed fire. Not for the first time Jane reflected that her friend was wasted in the female sex. She should have been able to take a seat in the House of Lords, where she could harangue the opposition to her heart's content.

"Ladies, let us face the facts. We have allowed ourselves to be cast adrift. We lack purpose. Direction. We must grasp the helm. Trim our sails. Set our course."

"Oh, for heaven's sake, Lavinia," Jane interrupted, "do get to the point before I become seasick."

"Very well, then. I have been considering our situation for some time now. Since the moment that I, by chance, met an elderly gentleman at the museum who quite inspired me. Like a certain ancient philosopher, he felt, you see, that the unexamined life is not worth living. His joie de vivre was most contagious. Although"—she interrupted herself in a reflective aside—"I could not share his enthusiasm for tittlebats."

"Tittlebats?" Addie inquired. "What on earth is a tittlebat?"

"I have not the slightest idea. But it seems that this Mr.—Pickford? Pickens?—well, the name escapes me now, but I do recall that the fact we shared the first syllable was a bond between us.

Anyhow, he had written a scholarly treatise on tittlebats. But let me get to the issue at hand."

"Pray do," Jane murmured.

"This gentleman, who is our senior, let me add, embraced a philosophy that I found inspiring. No, more than that. Enviable. And he and his friends, in order to incorporate his principles into their lives, have banded themselves into a club."

"Uh-oh," Jane commented into her teacup.

"Have formed a club," Lady Lavinia repeated for emphasis. "And from this organization's membership, he and three other gentlemen had been newly named the Corresponding Society. Their purpose is to enlarge their horizons. They plan extended travels during which they shall advance the perimeters of knowledge through an investigation of the character and manners of the people with whom they come in contact and from an analytical observation of the scenery and local customs. Well, you get the idea. The important thing is that they do not plan to travel with no higher purpose than their own amusement. What is more, they plan to keep written accounts of their observations."

"You did say 'Corresponding Society,'" Jane asked. "With whom do they correspond?"

"With the other members of their club, of course. Those who are forced to remain here in London. But that is beside the point. Pray allow me to finish."

"I'm not so sure it is beside the point." Jane, who was beginning to see the way Lavinia's mind was working, spoke mutinously. "But go ahead."

"What I am leading up to is this. I want us to emulate those worthy gentlemen. Perhaps not always in particular, but certainly in principle. For there is nothing in their high-minded aims that would prevent us as females from following their examples. In short, I think that we three should form our own club." She paused for dramatic effect and gazed from one friend to the other.

"Fine." Jane set down her cup and saucer with rattling emphasis. "And you may be the Corresponding Society and I shall be the member that stays put and reads what you have written."

"You will do nothing of the kind," Lavinia snapped. "You of all people need the stimulation of travel, Jane. You are allowing yourself to grow absolutely—matronly." The word rolled off Lavinia's tongue like an epithet.

"No need to be offensive. I readily admit that I am no longer a sylph-like girl."

"You have grown a bit stout of late, dear," Addie offered.

"Well, it's a pity, then, that I cannot lend you a few pounds, for you could certainly benefit—"

"Enough!" Lavinia rapped the tea table with her knuckles, then winced and rubbed them. "You both have proved my point with your petty bickering. We do need stimulation. We do need purpose. We are, indeed, going to travel. And"—she rose and walked back to the library table, where she picked up the map she had been studying—"I have already chosen our first port of call. We are going to Bath."

"To Bath!" The two friends spoke in unison.

"We are going to Bath to broaden our horizons? For stimulation and purpose?" Jane was incredulous.

"But, Lavinia," Addie wailed, "no one who is anyone ever goes to Bath!"

Chapter
Three

L ORD JEREMY PICKERING HAD CHOSEN THAT PARTICU-
lar morning to pay a duty call upon his aunt
Lavinia. Or, to be more precise, the visit was not so
much his choice as it was his father's. He had had
a letter from the earl saying that a long silence
from Grosvenor Street seemed rather ominous and
that Jeremy should take it upon himself to see
what the Holy Terror was up to these days and put
a stop to it.

Lord Jeremy found his father's directive naive in
the extreme. Though oddly fond of his fearsome
aunt and suspecting that she, in her own starchy
way, returned the sentiment, the very idea that he
could put a stop to any undertaking she set her
mind to was ludicrous. He might as well have been
asked to divert the Thames.

Moffatt's eyes lit with pleasure as he responded

to a rapid tattoo beaten out upon the shiny brass knocker. "Nice to see you, sir. It has been some time since your last visit."

"So my father reminds me." Lord Jeremy stepped inside and handed the butler his black top hat.

He was a personable young man, modishly dressed in a claret cutaway coat with a nipped-in waist, sleeves that were gathered large at the shoulders, and a velvet collar. Fawn trousers and waistcoat, highlighted by a spotted fawn cravat, completed his ensemble. He had sandy hair and sky-blue eyes and an easygoing charm that few could resist, his aunt Lavinia being perhaps the most impervious. Moffatt, who had known him since he was a toddler in leading strings, lacked this immunity.

"But it's beyond me," the young man continued, "why Pater gets into such a taking. If Aunt Lavinia wishes to see me, she'll send out a summons. And if she should need to see me, I am sure you'll let me know, won't you, Moffatt?" He gave the old man an affectionate smile.

"Of course, sir." The butler beamed.

Jeremy's eyes scanned the hall and took note of a pair of pelisses and two umbrellas at rest by the entryway. "My aunt is entertaining, I see."

"Oh, no, sir. It's only Miss Jane and Miss Adelaide. Her ladyship summoned them this morning. I'm sure they'll be delighted to see you, sir. They're in the library." He made a move in that direction to announce him.

"No, just a minute, Moffatt. Summoned them? Sounds serious."

"As to that, I could not say, sir." Moffatt did not

try to hide his disapproval. "Her ladyship did not see fit to disclose just why she needed to see her friends immediately. For she did stress, sir, that Joe should not dawdle, which is his inclination, but deliver her messages with all haste."

"Hmmm. Something important must be afoot for the triumvirate to be in session. I think I'll wait upstairs till the meeting breaks up. Let me know when, Moffatt, so I can greet the honorary aunts."

After Lord Jeremy had settled himself in the morning room, where he could watch the activity on the street below, a strong desire to blow a cloud almost overcame him. Knowing his aunt's strong disapproval of his "noxious habit," he weighed his tobacco craving against her wrath. The latter won out easily. At least it did at first. But as boredom lent its presence to the argument, Lord Jeremy hit on a possible solution. He would choose one of the unused bedchambers in which to smoke. And, well, if Aunt Lavinia did still manage to nose him out, he was, after all, a grown man now, ineligible to be jerked by the ear and perched upon a stool while she read him the riot act, as had happened on the first occasion when she had caught him engaged in that activity.

Upon opening the door to the yellow bedchamber and finding it occupied, Lord Jeremy's first instinct was to pass on to the blue room next door. But the sight of the chambermaid, bucket in one hand, rag in the other, standing on tiptoe and stretching far as possible in order to reach the top panes of the window, diverted him.

The locks of flaxen hair that had strayed from beneath the mobcap were curling in damp ringlets. The figure was neat and trim. The exposed ankles

20

shared those characteristics. Certainly the back view of this domestic bespoke youth, a novelty in this household. Lord Jeremy ambled closer for a better look.

It was never his intention to sneak up on the window washer. The fault lay entirely with the well-oiled hinges, the deep Aubusson carpet, and the absorption of the chambermaid with the task in hand. But when his lordship placed his hands upon the trim waist and lifted the lithesome woman around for a closer look, he was greeted by a startled shriek a mere split second before he was deluged by a pail of dirty water.

Lord Jeremy was at a loss to know which was more devastating, being doused by the soapy contents of a servant's bucket or gazing drippingly upward at the most gorgeous female he had ever seen. And also the most furious. "How dare you, sir!" she said, spitting.

All in all, he was reasonably quick in recovering his equilibrium. After pulling a handkerchief from his pocket and proceeding to mop his face, he actually managed to speak. "Oh, I say. I think the shoe is on the other foot, you know," he pointed out reasonably. "I'm the one who should be saying 'How dare you,' for I think you just possibly may have ruined a brand-new coat, the pride of my overcharging tailor." He paused to dab futilely at the claret shoulders with his already sodden handkerchief. "Don't you think you reacted a bit too hastily? I mean to say, there is no need to be quite so prickly."

It was obvious that the chambermaid did not agree. But she was also obviously working to abate her fury. Her accent was as thick with Billingsgate as with sarcasm when she replied. "Beg pardon, sir, I'm sure. I forgot for a moment, you see, that it's perfectly proper for a swell to paw a female servant as well as to scare 'er 'alf out of 'er wits."

"Paw a servant. Paw her!" Jeremy felt his dander begin to rise. He was unaccustomed to have anyone, let alone a green slip of a servant girl, gaze upon him with such utter scorn. "I merely turned you around to see what you looked like. I did not paw you. In fact, I did nothing to warrant being half drowned with the dirty, soapy contents of that bucket. But since you seem to have pronounced me guilty, well then, I think the crime should fit the punishment." So saying, he snatched her off the stool and into his arms and had planted an angry kiss upon her lips before she had sufficient time to jerk them away.

The bucket dropped with a clang. The maid's fingernails targeted his lordship's cheek but were intercepted by a quick, firm clasp of her wrist. Her rather small but quite stout boot contacted his trousered shin, but the kiss went on.

"Jeremy!"

An imperious command barked from the doorway. "Release her at once!"

His lordship's compliance was reflex. As was, no doubt, the slap that landed on his cheek once he'd obeyed.

Lady Lavinia surveyed the scene with disapproval. Mrs. Abingdon and Mrs. Osborne stood behind her, each peering across a shoulder. Their jaws were slack with shock.

Her ladyship strode into the room. "I should like private speech with you, Jeremy. But first a word to this young person."

22

The chambermaid seemed to pale a bit, but, except for that, she had a tight rein on her composure.

"I feel compelled to point out, Kitty, that you have mishandled this situation abominably."

"Yes, mum." The lovely eyes were focused upon the floor.

"Oh, I say, Aunt—" Lord Jeremy began, only to be silenced with a snapped "Do be quiet, Jeremy. I said that we would talk later!

"Now, Kitty, while I am not one of those feeble-minded females who consider men to be their superiors in all things, I do acknowledge that, in most cases, *physically* the male does have the edge. And certainly this is true in the case of yourself and my nephew here. You could not hope to hold your own fairly against his attack."

"Attack!" Lord Jeremy exploded. "Dammit all, Aunt Lavinia, I did not attack this girl."

"Oh, do be quiet.

"As I was saying, Kitty, you cannot hope to overcome a stronger opponent by the methods you employed. And in view of the way you look and the base nature of most men (she ignored her nephew's glare), you have to learn to expect this sort of thing and be prepared to deal with it.

"Now, I will not say that dumping your bucket of water upon Jeremy was a mistake," she conceded. "One should always make do with the weapon at hand. And there are, possibly, a few men whose ardor would be extinguished by such a tactic. My nephew, obviously, is not of their number."

"Aunt Lavinia, is there a point to all of this?"

"There most certainly is. And if you cannot be

quiet and allow me to make it, please withdraw to the library."

"No, indeed. I would not miss a word of your battle plan." He folded his arms across his soaked chest and returned his aunt's haughty stare in kind.

"As I was saying, Kitty, making use of the weapon in your hand was strategically sound. While unlikely to stop your attacker cold, it could have bought you time to take to your heels and escape."

"Yes, mum."

"But positioned as you were next to a window too high to jump from and with the enemy between you and the door, the chances of your being able to get away were slim indeed. But still, the soapy water was worth the try. I congratulate you upon that bit of resourcefulness."

"Oh, for God's sake!" Jeremy exclaimed.

"Thank 'ee, mum." The corners of the maid's mouth twitched slightly.

"But where you failed dismally"—Lavinia walked farther into the room, trailed by her two friends—"was that once captured, you resorted to those feeble, ineffectual lines of resistance common to the female sex. First, I saw you try to scratch his cheek. He, expecting such a response—from past experience I presume (Jeremy glared again)—easily thwarted that attempt. Then, once released, due entirely to our intervention and not your own efforts I must needs point out, you employed the old female cliché of slapping the gentleman's face. Except for venting one's displeasure, that tactic is a total waste of time. It has no effect whatsoever upon the man.

"Now, my dear, let me show you what you should have done. First, being both victim and a member of the weaker sex, you must discard all previous notions of fair play and propriety. Your objective is to put a powerful attacker out of commission immediately. This is how it is done, Kitty. Pray, pay attention.

"Jeremy," she commanded, "come here and put your arms around me in the fashion you just employed."

"I will do no such thing."

"Jeremy!" Lavinia leveled him with a look. "I think you owe this young person a chance to learn how to defend herself. Whereas I realize that you meant her no real harm—"

"Well, thank you for that, Aunt Lavinia."

"Sarcasm does not become you, Jeremy. As I was saying, whereas you would not have ill-used her, her beauty makes her the natural target for those less-principled members of your sex. So grab me, Jeremy. I promise not to hurt you."

"I can't tell you how relieved that makes me." He grinned suddenly. 'Oh, very well."

Jeremy ambled over and seized his aunt, pinning her arms tightly to her sides. Her knee came up like lightning, pausing just below his crotch.

"Good God!" His face was frozen in shock as he released her. Behind them, Addie and Jane gasped.

"You see, Kitty"—Lavinia turned toward the astonished chambermaid and concluded her lecture— "you must strike the male where he is most vulnerable. If my knee had made contact with my nephew's—"

"Lavinia!" Addie and Jane chorused in horror.

"He would now be writhing on the floor, hors de

combat, allowing you sufficient time to make good your escape. Remember that, Kitty."

"Yes, Lady Lavinia." The chambermaid bobbed her head and placed a hand over her mouth to hide the dimples that had appeared. But a smothered giggle betrayed her.

A bit later, Lord Jeremy, his muscular shoulders draped in Lady Lavinia's dressing gown while the servants tended to his coat and linen, was seated across from his aunt in the morning room. He had a restoring cup of steaming tea in his hand. A heaping plate of scones was set before him. He was not, however, mollified. The look he bent upon his relative was censorious in the extreme.

"You are hard, Aunt Lavinia," he observed. "Not even to mention lacking in all female delicacy."

"Fustian. What does 'delicacy' have to say in the matter? A woman needs to know how to protect herself, especially those young and personable targets of masculine lust. And I simply pointed out the most expedient manner of doing so."

Jeremy shuddered. "You most certainly did. Never mind leaving a cove impotent. After all, you have no need to concern yourself about the family name being carried on. My brother Horace has seen to that."

"Do not exaggerate. And do not forget that you did bring all this upon yourself. Now, shall we drop the matter? Why not tell me the real purpose of your visit. For I do not suppose you stopped by merely to seduce my chambermaid. You are in a financial difficulty perhaps?"

He put down his cup and glared. "Now, that stings, b'gad. Once, just once, I did apply to you for help when I was all to pieces. I was a mere fourteen, as I recall."

"And had been gulled by a cardsharp and were afraid to ask your father for the funds."

"Yes, and you were a trump about the whole affair," he admitted grudgingly. "You never squeaked beef on me. But you will admit I have not approached you for money since then. Besides, do I have to have a reason for a family visit?"

"Well, yes," she retorted. "Your most redeeming quality, Jeremy, is that, unlike your father, you are quite content to lead your own life and allow me to lead mine. Since we've disposed of the money factor, which I grant I found an unlikely motive for your visit, I can now assume that Newbright has hectored you into checking on me."

"Well, he does tend to take his brotherly responsibilities seriously. And he claims to have written you twice with no reply and hence was worried. Though why he should concern himself about you is beyond me. Attila the Hun, I suspect, was less self-sufficient."

"Now, now. Bitterness does not become you," she reproached him while still appearing to take his put-down as a tribute. "And if it will make amends, I promise to write Newbright a reassuring letter and apprise him of the fact that you have done your duty.

"Ah, are his lordship's things dry, Mary?" The maid had appeared at the open doorway.

"Yes, your ladyship. They look good as new, sir. No thanks to some," she added darkly.

When Jeremy surveyed himself in the cheval glass of the blue bedchamber moments later, he had to agree. He was very much the Bond Street

27

beau again. It was amazing how being bang-up-to-the-nines could restore a cove's equilibrium. Still, his conscience tended to niggle a bit in spite of the fact that the pretty chambermaid had given more than she got. What's more, her position was not in jeopardy. She had had nothing but approval from his aunt. But Jeremy was well aware that her fellow servants were not so democratic in their outlook. They were likely to make the young girl's life miserable for dumping her dirty water upon a nob.

A glance in the yellow room found it empty. He moved on to his aunt's bedchamber. The maid was on her stool again, attacking the small rectangular windowpanes with her rag. Jeremy prudently cleared his throat.

"Don't even think it." He gestured toward the bucket as he entered. "I'm here to beg your pardon. Oh, my soul, you've been crying. I say, I am terribly sorry. You won't believe this, but I'm not really in the habit—oh, God, I almost could wish you had applied Aunt Lavinia's technique."

She nearly smiled at that.

"Please forgive me—Kitty, is it? And I will have a word with Moffatt before I leave, saying that this whole soapy-water business was all my fault. I practically begged to be doused."

She looked alarmed. "Oh, no, sir. Pray don't do that."

"Why not? He did rake you over the coals, didn't he?"

"Well, yes. But you taking me part, sir, would only make things worse. Not only with Mr. Moffatt, but with the other servants as well."

"I see." As he recalled plain, lumpy Mary and the advanced age and ordinary looks of the rest of the staff, he could well imagine that this exquisite was as out of place as a bird of paradise among a flock of sparrows. "Well, I won't say anything if you'd rather I did not. But at least tell me that I'm forgiven."

Jeremy's winning smile was wont to smooth his path through life. This time its effect was nil.

"There is nothing to forgive, sir" was the frigid answer. "Servants do not expect to be treated same as gentry." She turned then and vigorously reapplied her rag to the window.

He stared at her forbidding back a moment, then left to clatter down the stairs and, with the briefest of nods to Moffatt, who sprang to open the door for him, emerged into the horse-scented air of Grosvenor Street.

"Damn Father, anyhow," he muttered as he hurried along, twanging the bars of the fences with his cane like so many cast-iron harp strings. "This is the last time he'll persuade me to spy on Aunt Lavinia. She can go to the devil in her own curst way."

Why he had found the visit so upsetting was, for the moment, quite beyond him. Jeremy was not one to refine overly much upon his dignity. So it was not the reflex dousing that bothered him. Ergo it must be something about the chambermaid herself. Two memories flooded back, causing him to come to an abrupt halt, to his peril, while crossing Oxford Street. First, there was the earth-shaking sensation of that stolen kiss. And, second, came the realization that the initial words he had heard from those lovely lips had been uttered in accents at least as aristocratic as his own.

Chapter
Four

THE ORGANIZATIONAL MEETING HAD NOT PROCEEDED as smoothly as the founder of the new club might have wished. The problem was that Lavinia Pickering's two oldest and dearest friends had proved annoyingly recalcitrant. It was as though, Jane had remarked earlier in private to Addie, the Christians, while knowing that their grizzly fate was inevitable, were still determined to give the lion indigestion.

The meeting took place in Mrs. Abingdon's small but tastefully furnished withdrawing room. The founder's first objection was to holding a business meeting around a tea table, her next to the lavish spread the hostess had provided for their refreshment. There was tea, of course, and a pot of chocolate accompanied by a wide variety of cakes. The repast was served upon the hostess's finest china.

"Oh, for heaven's sake, Jane," Lavinia snapped, "this is a business meeting. That is what I most dislike about our sex," she lectured as she served her plate with nun's cake, two queen cakes, and six gingerbread nuts. "We are incapable of behaving like our male counterparts. Everything we do must be turned into a frivolity."

"Why, that is not so," Addie retorted. "My own dear Lieutenant Oliver" (here her eyes grew moist, as they always did at the mention of her late husband, even though that unfortunate gentleman had shuffled off his mortal coil nearly thirty years before) "spoke often of the honor of being asked to take tea with his colonel, even when the regiment was on the move. And surely you do not consider the army frivolous, Lavinia."

"Well, I doubt they used a silver service," Lady Lavinia countered as she offered her cup to Mrs. Abingdon for a refill.

"As a matter of fact, the dear lieutenant did mention the monogrammed—"

"Never mind!" Lavinia cut through the military reminiscence with accustomed authority. "Let us proceed with the matter at hand. And our first order of business should be to give our club a suitable name."

"Why?" Jane passed the plate of cakes to Addie, who took a pepper cake, then thoughtfully exchanged it for a gingerbread nut. "The three of us have been doing things together all our lives without a title. Why should a trip to Bath be so different?"

"Do not be an obstructionist. You know very well why. As I explained when I first broached the subject, we are about to found a society that has the potential for wide expansion. When they learn of our objectives, serious-minded women everywhere will wish to join our ranks. This movement might well spread throughout the kingdom."

"Oh, not the globe?"

"Wherever the Union Jack flies. Why not? So it behooves us to think carefully before deciding upon a name. Our title should reflect our purpose. For instance, we might call ourselves the Observers of Life Club. Or the O.L.C. for short."

"Hmmm." Jane mulled the suggestion over carefully. "I see. Or why not the Female Observers of Life Society. Or the F.O.O.L.S. for short."

Before Lavinia could deliver the scathing setdown so obviously forming upon her lips, Addie quickly interposed a suggestion that their organization be known simply as the Pickering Club. And even though the founder modestly opposed the idea, it was very plain to see that she was pleased. Jane, who was feeling a bit ashamed of her negative attitude, quickly moved that the organization be so named. Addie seconded and it was unanimously decided.

There was, of course, no question but that Lady Lavinia should be president of the new society. And she overrode Jane's opinion that the embryo organization needed no further officers. "You will be secretary pro tem," she stated firmly. "It is of the utmost importance that our business be recorded." Then, since Addie was beginning to bristle at the notion of being the only ranker left in the organization, she quickly appointed her treasurer. And once assured that in point of fact there would be no money to take care of, Addie promptly accepted the honor.

"The next order of business is our scientific expedition to Bath, which will take place the day after tomorrow."

This undemocratic declaration was met with consternation. "I can't possibly be ready by then," Addie wailed while Jane chorused, "Are you out of your mind?"

"There is little need for preparation. You will be taking only fourteen pounds of luggage. As for our departure date, that is not open to negotiation. I have already booked four seats upon the Bath coach for us."

"You've done what?" the other two exclaimed. Their faces were as unanimous as their tone in reflecting horror. "Has something happened to your traveling coach?" Addie asked.

"No, of course not. My carriage is in perfect working order. But you two seem to have forgotten the purpose of our organization. Our aim is to explore new experiences. Has either one of you ever availed yourself of public transportation?"

"Certainly not!"

Addie contented herself with an expressive shudder.

"I rest my case."

"Just a minute." Jane was recovering enough to recall Lavinia's statement in its entirety. "You did say four places? Whose is the other one?"

Lavinia tried, unsuccessfully, to sound offhand. "Oh, I reserved that for my personal maid."

"And I suppose our maids will be coming in your well-sprung, luxurious carriage while we bounce around with the hoi polloi." Adelaide spoke with no little bitterness.

"No. My carriage will remain in the carriage house. No servants will be going."

"None but Mary, you mean. We are expected to explore the new experience of doing without our maids while you take Mary along. Why, I'll wager you're using up her fourteen pounds worth of luggage weight as well. You'll have all your best gowns in Bath while Jane and I will be obliged to look like dowds."

"I am not taking any more than my own allotted weight. In fact, I do not envision the need of that much luggage. Which brings me to the next order of business—our club uniform."

She bent over to retrieve a covered basket that she had led her friends to believe contained needlework. This had struck the two as rather odd, since Lavinia never engaged in that pursuit. They now eyed the basket suspiciously.

"I have taken the liberty of designing the sort of garment that will be imminently better suited to our new mode of life than the clothes we are accustomed to wear. You have often heard me express my views on the restrictions of female clothing. And why our sex should be hampered by skirts— hampered? *hobbled* would be the mot juste—while gentlemen are free to stride, to run, to jump, to ride, is a question that cries out for consideration."

Jane gazed at her friend with dark suspicion growing upon her face while Addie groped beneath her chair and fished out her reticule. From it she produced a small bottle of sal volatile which she held at the ready.

Rather like a conjurer promising to produce a rabbit from a hat, Lavinia stretched the suspense. "You may recall my strong views upon the subject of Lady Caroline Lamb when she was making a cake of herself years ago over that libertine poet. So while I strongly disapprove of—"

"Oh, for heaven's sake, Lavinia, what does Caroline Lamb have to say to anything!" Jane interrupted in exasperation. "Do get on with this uniform thing."

"I simply wished to give credit where credit is due." Lady Lavinia was very much upon her dignity. "When I said just now that I have designed a uniform for us, that is not strictly true. What I have done is to adapt the garment affected by Lady Caroline when she used to follow that Gordon fellow around while dressed as a pageboy."

"Ooooh," Addie moaned faintly, opening the sal volatile. She inhaled deeply.

Lady Lavinia dipped into the basket and produced a garment. She held it up for their inspection.

There was a stunned silence. "Oh, my word," Jane breathed.

The garment, constructed from pomegranate-colored gros de Naples fabric checked with black and a deeper shade of pomegranate, resembled a pair of voluminous trousers. It was gathered in the waist, divided for the limbs, and, once more, gathered at the ankles.

Jane recovered first. "Are you sure that you do not have your sources confused," she remarked tartly. "That must have been inspired by a Turkish harem."

"Nothing—*nothing*," Addie chimed in faintly, "will induce me to wear that. It is obscene."

"Ridiculous!" Lavinia snorted. "It is nothing of the kind. You are both so hidebound in convention

35

that you fail to see that my garment is by far more modest than that gown you are wearing, Adelaide. You cannot climb a tree, take a tumble, or run across a field without violating that very modesty you value so highly. Whereas in this garment"—she waved the pomegranate trousers like a flag—"one can do any of those things with no fear of putting oneself to the blush."

"I personally have no intention of climbing any trees or racing across fields at my age," Jane glared.

"You do not intend to do so, but who knows when the vicissitudes—" There was something in Jane's expression that caused her friend to change her tack. "Oh, never mind the extraordinary circumstances. It is the everyday occurrences I particularly had in mind. Think, for instance, how you could mount into a carriage without a gaggle of male loiterers ogling your ankles."

"No one has ogled my ankles for over twenty years," Jane snapped. "And were I to climb into a carriage in that garment, any gaggle of males would either be in a state of shock or rolling upon the ground, howling with laughter."

"Pray try and withhold your judgment until you have seen the rest of the uniform," Lavinia said frostily. "Now then." She produced for their inspection a smocklike overgarment of solid pomegranate, gathered voluminously upon a square yoke, with long sleeves and a rufflike collar. "This will go over our pantaloons," she informed the two rigid ladies, "and fall well below the knees. Now, I ask you, could anything be more proper?"

"Lady Lavinia." Jane's look was repressive, her tone recalcitrant. "There is no way that I am going to appear in public clad like some superannuated refugee from a seraglio. And if doing so is requisite to becoming a member of the Pickering Club, I here and now tender my resignation."

"Me, too."

There was a long and pregnant pause while the leader eyed her mutinous followers. It was touch-and-go as the black eyes sparked and a look of contempt played upon the aristocratic features. But then she released a long, shuddering sigh of martyrdom and returned the controversial uniform to its basket. "You disappoint me. You do, indeed, disappoint me. But then, I tell myself, this is the very attitude that illustrates the need for a club for females such as ours. Ladies, your outlook is in dire need of expansion. You must strive to strip yourselves of your narrow, conventional views and learn to live free. I do not despair. For I dare to predict that your attitudes will shortly undergo a sea change, that our club experiences will enable you to shed your provincialism and see the world with fresh new eyes."

"In Bath?" Jane inquired with sweet cynicism.

"Fustian!" Addie added.

But she took care to muffle the comment with her handkerchief.

Chapter
Five

"IT WILL NOT DO, YOU KNOW."

Lady Lavinia had been sitting with unaccustomed patience in front of her dressing table, peering into the glass while Kitty worked with her hair. She had watched the lovely reflected face, the lower lip sucked between the perfect teeth, become a mask of frustrated intensity. The goal had been to achieve a modish look. The results might have been accomplished by a drunken farmer with a hay fork.

The girl stood back to view the coiffure from a different perspective. It did not help. Her expression was a mixture of horror and despair. "Oh, dear. It ain't quite right, is it, mum?" The cockney vowels cascaded off her tongue. "But I'm sure it just needs a touch here and there to set it all to rights."

"No, Kitty." Lady Lavinia spoke firmly as she

picked up the brush and attacked the sausage curls that almost concealed the fiery mark left upon her cheek by the curling tongs. "It is quite obvious that you have never done anyone's hair before."

"But I could learn, mum." She pleaded. "I'm ever so willing."

"I am sure you could, Kitty." Lady Lavinia managed to give her voice a conviction that she did not feel. "Just as I am sure that given time, you could learn to make a bed properly. But upon consideration, I have concluded that both endeavors would only put you and the household through unnecessary anguish. For it becomes more and more evident that you are not cut out to be either a chambermaid or an abigail."

Her voice shook ever so slightly as Kitty asked, "Does that mean I'm dismissed, mum?"

"What it means is that I need to reconsider your position. I had thought to palm you off on our excursions as my personal maid. But that will not do. It was a bad idea anyway," she conceded with unaccustomed grace. "For my two friends have their noses out of joint because their maids are not coming. And Mary, who has been with me practically all our lives, is going around looking like St. Sebastian sans his arrows and threatening to seek employment with my brother. 'His lordship knows the worth of old family retainers,' " she mimicked.

"No, Kitty, you simply are not up to snuff as a servant. You shall have to become a relation. God knows it does not require any degree of skill to be one of those."

"M-mum?" Kitty was staring at Lady Lavinia's reflection as if doubting her mistress's sanity or her own hearing.

"Yes, it is decided. You shall come along. By the bye, I am right, am I not, that you were overjoyed at the prospect of leaving London? I thought so," she said with satisfaction as the girl nodded. "Well then, you shall be a relation. And a junior member of the Pickering Club. So that is settled." Lady Lavinia picked up her white cap from the dressing table and set it firmly upon the now-smooth dark hair. "Be ready to depart at a quarter past six tomorrow morning. That should give us ample time."

"Yes, mum."

Lady Lavinia sighed. "I do not think you quite understand, my dear. You can now, thank God, rid yourself of that dreadful Drury Lane mode of speech. And," she mused, "*Kitty* no longer seems suitable. You shall be called Catherine. Catherine Pickering. Is that agreeable?"

"I—I think so, mu—er, Lady Lavinia." The young girl gazed at the older woman nervously.

"Oh, you need not be alarmed, m'dear. I have no intention of probing into your personal affairs. Of course, if you choose to tell me just why it is that you, a lady—which, by the bye, was instantly apparent to me at the servants' registry—are reduced to your present circumstances, I shall be most happy to hear your explanation." She waited expectantly.

There was a long-drawn-out pause while "Catherine" seemed to be weighing the matter.

"Pray forgive me, Lady Lavinia," she finally replied in a soft and cultured voice, "but I collect it would be best if I did not. I should not wish to be the cause of a troubled conscience."

If consulted, her ladyship's closest friends might have pointed out that the likelihood of her suffering that particular discomfort was slim indeed. But Lavinia herself did not argue. "I see," she replied. "I may take it for granted, I presume, that you have done nothing of a criminal nature?"

"Oh, no, your ladyship."

"Well then. Go on to bed, child. Our adventures begin in the morning."

Mrs. Abingdon and Mrs. Oliver were the first of the Pickering Club to arrive at the White Horse Cellar. They had come by hackney coach and Addie, despite the muggy, depressing drizzle, stuck her head out the window to gaze around her with apprehension. She found the prospects decidedly offputting. Coaches were leaving and arriving at what she considered most alarming speeds, their horses steaming in the dampness. Vendors of all kinds were shouting for attention. Watch guards and toasting forks, pencil cases and sponges, competed with a penknife that boasted so many blades for so many different purposes that the chance of their ever fitting back into their appointed slots seemed remote indeed. Newspaper sellers hawked their soggy wares, and Addie drew back in alarm as an orange vendor thrust a dripping specimen of overripe fruit underneath her nose. "Lavinia is not here," she reported. "Perhaps she has changed her mind."

"Nonsense. Did you ever know her to withdraw from any of her scatterbrained schemes?"

"Did you ever know her to be late?"

That was something of a leveler, but Jane rallied. "Well, actually, she isn't late. It is merely seven. We have a full half hour before the coach is due to leave."

"But she ordered us to arrive a little before seven. I tell you, she has changed her mind. I shall tell the driver to take us home."

"You will do nothing of the sort. Come on."

The jarvey, who had been in no hurry to leave his perch, climbed down too late to open the door for the ladies. A pack of porters swooped down upon their luggage and began to snarl at one another for the privilege of seeing to it.

"I suppose we had best go inside." Jane spoke with some annoyance as she raised an umbrella against the drizzle. "If Lavinia considers this a kind of test—making us cope on our own when we wanted no part of this business—well, I shall certainly have a thing or two to say when—" She stopped abruptly, her mouth agape. And at the same instant all noise and animation in the busy yard seemed to cease.

An elderly "pageboy" had just dismounted from a hackney and, followed by a younger version of the type, was headed purposefully toward them. "Oh, dear heaven, she's wearing it." Jane gasped faintly while Addie thought of reentering their coach but was too weak-kneed to accomplish it.

The uniform of the Pickering Club, which had seemed merely bizarre when held up for inspection, now appeared scandalous. From the knee down, the presence of limbs was appallingly apparent. Of course the garments did allow freedom of movement. Jane admitted as much, silently to herself. Lavinia was not walking, she was striding, while the young person struggled to keep up. Their smocks seemed to spread like sails away from their bodies and the drizzle hardly made an impression upon their headgear.

"Oh, would you look at what they have on their heads," Addie found enough voice to croak.

"I am looking," Jane said grimly. "I am sure that my son Robert had something just like it when he was five."

The two approaching ladies were wearing black caps made of soft leather. Their crowns were wide and low. Black tassels danced rakishly across narrow bills just above the left eyes of the wearers.

"She didn't show us those," Addie said weakly.

"She would not have dared."

"Oh, Lavinia, how could you?" Addie accused her friend as soon as the two joined them.

Lady Lavinia chose to misinterpret the charge. "I do apologize for being late. There had to be some adjustments made in Catherine's costume. I had overestimated her stature. Her smock needed shortening."

Catherine's cheeks were suffused with pink as she tried to ignore the titters (and now a few male whistles) that their progress across the inn yard had provoked. She had been too grateful to her benefactress to balk at wearing an outfit that she considered best suited to the pantomime. But now, with so much attention being focused upon them, she was beginning to wonder if on the whole she would not prefer to be washing windows.

Lady Lavinia produced a man's watch from a pocket she had incorporated into her garment. "Actually, I see that we still have a full twenty-five minutes until our departure. That gives us time for a bracing cup of tea."

The whistles and hoots increased as the quartet made its way to the inn door. Lady Lavinia's lofty expression conveyed the message that she was oblivious of such discourtesy. The newly christened Catherine Pickering tried to follow her mentor's example, but to her dismay she could feel her cheeks burn hotter.

Their entrance into the crowded traveler's room created no less a stir. Most patrons simply stared. But a travel-weary merchant elbowed a sleeping companion next to him on the settle, causing the man to cut a snore off in mid-crescendo and then sit upright and gape. The waiter behind a wooden counter froze in the act of trying to clean the ale remnants out of a glass with an unappetizing towel.

As Lavinia led the way to an alcove table, she called out an order of tea and toast for four. "Do make haste," she said, frowning at the still-paralyzed waiter. "We should like to have it before the Bath coach leaves.

"Now then." After they were seated, she riveted her two friends with a steady, guileless gaze. "I expect that I owe you an explanation for Catherine's presence. You both seemed to take umbrage when I announced that I was taking a personal maid upon an expedition designed to change our customary mode of living. Well, I cannot blame you for your attitude. So let me set the record straight. Young Catherine here—Miss Pickering, that is to say—is not a servant of any kind. She is, in fact, a distant cousin of mine who for reasons of her own"—she paused to underscore that point—"preferred to remain incognito. But I have persuaded her to drop a pose that I suspect"—here she looked pointedly at Jane—"fooled no one. I particularly thought it safe to abandon the charade since Catherine has never been to Bath. I am right about that, am I not, m'dear?"

"Why, yes. But how did you know?"

"No one under fifty ever goes to Bath?" Jane theorized.

During a silence while the waiter served their tea, Addie was thinking furiously. "Your cousin?" she said once he had left them. "But I cannot imagine. She would have to be one of the Sussex Pickerings, I collect. But the only ones of those I ever saw were not fair. They were quite dark, in fact. More like you, Lavinia. Though come to think on it, your cousin Ivor did marry a woman who—"

"Never mind," Lavinia cut in sharply. "There is no need to shake the family tree, Adelaide. I have said that Catherine is a distant cousin. This applies to geography as well as genealogy. She has lived abroad all her life."

Catherine suddenly choked on her buttered toast. It took several sips of tepid tea to set her to rights. She looked warily at Lady Lavinia for clues to an apparent omniscience.

"Well now, I can see that we are making our young friend uncomfortable with this attention." Lavinia firmly brought the subject to a close. "It is enough to know that she is my cousin, under my protection, and a neophyte member of the newly formed Pickering Club."

Once again she produced the gold watch from its pocket and snapped open the gold case. "The coach should be departing in five minutes. Ladies, shall we go?"

Chapter
Six

WHILE THE BATH STAGE LOADED ITS PASSENGERS and luggage, Lady Lavinia could not resist giving her closest friends an I-told-you-so look. "Catherine and I will take the outside seats," she announced, "since we, unlike you, are sensibly dressed to mount to the top of the carriage. Fortunately, I have reserved two seats inside."

"If you actually expect me to take this journey with you," Jane replied, "that is fortunate." And Addie added with a trembling voice, "I would not climb to the top of that carriage even if I were wearing a hussar's uniform."

Lady Lavinia climbed up unassisted, just to prove that she could do so. Catherine joined her "cousin" in their rooftop perch just behind the driver and a soldier going home on leave. Jane and Addie squeezed inside the coach, where they became two extra persons in a compartment designed for four.

Since Addie was known to be a poor traveler, Jane had seen to it that her friend should face forward in the coach. As they made their way by fits and starts through the heavy London traffic, she watched with some anxiety as Addie's face took on a greenish cast. She was relieved to see her complexion return to a more healthy hue once the coach had reached the Kensington turnpike.

The respite was short-lived. They had covered only a few miles, when a corpulent gentleman, who was overextended into the space allotted Addie, produced a cigar and lighted it. One strong pull and exhalation sent a cloud of smoke throughout the carriage. Addie's color instantly grew alarming.

The farmer seated next to Jane pointedly lowered the window light. But the damp air did little to dispel the noxious cloud. Nor did Jane's glare give the corpulent gentleman any second thoughts about his behavior. Obviously the situation called for stronger action. What would Lavinia do in a case like this? Jane asked herself, then lacked the courage to snatch the cigar from between the pudgy fingers and toss it out the window. Instead, "Sir," she said politely, "would you mind extinguishing your cigar? I fear that the smoke is making my friend ill."

The man gave Jane an assessing look. "Cross patch" was apparently his verdict. He then twisted his massive body in order to peer down at Adelaide. She was leaning as far away from him as possible to the discomfort of a young man trying to sleep. "Can't this little lady speak for herself?" he asked. "I say, madam," he boomed down at the female cowering beside him, "you don't mind if I smoke me cheroot, now, do you? Man's got to do something to pass the time, don't you know. Dashed tedious, these coach trips. Almost finished anyhow. Shame to waste a good cigar. What do you say, ma'am?"

Addie, much to Jane's disgust, gave the smoker a weak smile that he took for permission. After a hard look at Jane that seemed to reconfirm his original assessment, he went back to the enjoyment of his cigar. He did, however, condescend to blow his smoke in the direction of the window. But since this served only to waft it back into the coach again, it was a useless attempt at courtesy.

"Adelaide dear," Jane said sweetly, "if you are about to cast up your accounts, would you please direct it into the gentleman's lap?"

The man turned to glare at the speaker and by chance glanced down at her companion. Addie's green was now the deep shade of pond scum. Her handkerchief was clapped over her mouth.

"Oh, gads! Here now. Hold on, little lady." The cigar shot out the window with a fiery streak. "Don't give in. Think of something else. That always works for me. And here now. You take the window seat." He was scrambling across Addie's lap, treading heavily on her toes in the process. The ensuing pain served as a diversion from her internal woes. "Now then, m'dear, lean your head well out there and think of apple blossoms."

There was fresh air aplenty on top of the coach. Catherine was surprised to discover that she enjoyed experiencing the world from such a lofty perch. She was even growing tolerant of her costume, forced to concede that its designer was right, she was accorded an ease of movement that might indeed spoil her afterward for confining skirts. And she had to admire the manner in which her companion disposed of the leers launched her way from several of the male passengers who shared their perch. One imperious glance had squelched both ridicule and familiarity.

The farther removed she became from London, the more her spirits lifted. Servant status had been a blow to her pride. Unbidden, the memory of an impudent male face laughing up at her while a strong hand grasped her ankle came flooding back. She was deeply grateful to Lady Lavinia for rescuing her from that sort of humiliation. And she was beginning to suspect that in addition to being unconventional, autocratic, and imperious, Lavinia Pickering was a very kindhearted woman indeed.

The sound of a rapidly approaching carriage broke into Catherine's reveries. She glanced at the road behind to see what sort of vehicle was overtaking them. A horse lover, she focused first upon the perfectly matched pair of high-stepping grays. Then, as her gaze traveled upward to take in the privileged owner of such superb cattle, she gave a slight gasp and froze. It took all her strength of resolve to turn her head casually forward and pull her cap bill farther down to shield her face as though protecting her eyes from the faint rays of the sun that were at last beginning to hold their own with the clouds and mist. She kept a hand upon the cap's bill, as though to anchor it fast. Her arm concealed her face from the passing carriage.

The precaution was unnecessary. The curricle driver had not a glance to spare for the public conveyance as he skillfully guided his pair past it on a stretch of road narrow enough to cause the coach passengers to hold their collective breaths and the coachman to fling a string of oaths at the rapidly diminishing carriage.

Lady Lavinia had not missed her young charge's reaction. Therefore, she had spared no glance for the elegant equipage nor any anxiety for the mere hairbreadth between the two vehicles. All her attention was focused upon the driver.

She saw a scowling, handsome man, nearing thirty, so she judged, with dark hair showing beneath his beaver. He had a long and narrow face with a pronounced cleft in the outthrust chin. His dark eyes were narrowed as he accurately gauged the distance between coach and curricle.

He was not a young gentleman one would soon forget, she concluded as she formed an instantaneous dislike, based, of course, upon her ability to read character in the physiognomy rather than upon her protégé's odd reaction.

Only two more things, of small note, happened to break the tedium of the remainder of the trip. Inside, the corpulent gentleman had grown quite solicitous of Addie's well-being, and much to the disgust of the driver and the other passengers kept them standing for several minutes at a posting house while he fetched her a restoring cup of tea.

Outside, Lavinia grew more and more disapproving as she observed that their coachman tended, at every opportunity, to fortify himself from a bottle concealed within his caped, voluminous coat. Then, when they did make a lengthy stop for a greatly overpriced and decidedly inferior meal, her ladyship watched with narrowed eyes as he flirted with a barmaid, who rewarded his banter by constantly refilling his ale mug. Therefore, when it came time to take their places in and on the coach again, the coachman, who had been the last to leave (since he required several moments to properly buss the barmaid) found his place taken by a grim and determined lady clad in harem trousers.

"Look'ee 'ere, move over, ma'am," he barked.

"You are in no condition to control these horses, sir" was the imperious reply.

"That's a damned slander," he blustered. "Been driving this route for near fifteen years now without a spill."

"If that is so, your guardian angel must be exhausted. You, sir, are foxed. I will not allow you to put all our lives in jeopardy. I intend to drive. You may sit beside me and sleep off your intoxication."

"When hell freezes over!" the driver pronounced thickly. "I'm not turning over my coach to any bedlamite female who ain't even got the common decency to wear skirts."

"My attire has nothing to say to the matter. The fact remains that you are unfit to drive, whereas I now know precisely how to proceed. (Indeed, she had studied his every movement with the intent of recording his technique in the club notes under the heading: How to Drive a Coach.) So take your place, sir."

The only passengers in a position to observe and overhear this exchange were Catherine and the young guardsman who had originally been seated beside the driver. Lavinia had had no difficulty in effecting an exchange. The soldier was not at all loathe to trade the uncouth coachman for a beautiful young lady. They watched in fascination as her ladyship ended the argument by pressing a sovereign into the coachman's outstretched palm.

Lady Lavinia's severest critic would never accuse her of a lack of confidence. Mindful of the time they had lost and desiring to impress the muttering coachman, she chose to spring her cattle. The art of snaking a long whip far out over the backs of four horses and then cracking it in the leader's ear was much easier in principle, she discovered, than execution. What she actually accomplished was to hit the off-animal on the rump. The effect, however, was similar to the one she had hoped for. That animal reared, then bolted. The others had no choice but to follow. The coach lunged forward while the outside passengers clung to the seat rails for dear life and the unwary insiders piled upon one another. The passage through the narrow courtyard entrance was a near thing indeed, causing the coachman to change his stream of protesting oaths into a fervent prayer.

But once the runaway coach-and-four had left the scattering village traffic behind and was dashing down a straight stretch of highway, the horses lost their panic in the familiar. It was therefore a smug and triumphant Lady Lavinia who, as dusk was about to overtake them, guided her cattle, with a modicum of skill, into the busy courtyard of the White Hart Inn at Bath.

Chapter
Seven

*L*ORD JEREMY PICKERING WAS KNOWN FOR HIS ROSY
outlook. His disposition as a rule was sunny. He
himself could come up with no logical reason for the
case of blue devils he had been suffering of late. His
friends, noting the change, privately speculated that
old Jeremy must have fallen in love at last. Only a female could mess up a cove's equilibrium in just that
way. Had anyone been brave enough to voice this the-
ory to Lord Jeremy, they would have received a terse
"Fustian!" and a set-down look for their pains.

His lordship was not one, however, to give in to his
misery. He had continued, after his encounter with
the prickly upstairs maid, to haunt White's Club for
Gentlemen on St. James's Street. But for some
strange reason, he had not found the company as ex-
hilarating as formerly. He therefore welcomed the diversion, late one evening, when his closest friend,

Lord Crews, interrupted a boring game of whist by glancing up from his cards to gasp, "My word! You won't believe who just walked in. Don't look, though."

Four necks instantly craned in the direction of the doorway.

What the four pairs of eyes saw was a glowering young man with the incipient marks of dissipation just beginning to line his handsome face. As the fierce eyes swung their way, the whist players speedily shifted their own to study their cards intently.

"Who was that?" the greenest player, young Phillip Chase, whispered after the angry young man had stridden past them to the faro table on the opposite side of the enormous room.

"You mean you don't know?" Crews looked astounded in that superior way that delights in another's ignorance. "That's Lord Monkhouse. 'Monk' to his friends."

"Friends? Didn't know he had any. Don't you mean 'to his enemies'?" The fourth player, a massive young man, chuckled as he led a card.

"Them, too, Clarence." Crews acknowledged the hit. "A most disagreeable cove, actually. Best to steer clear of him."

"Believe me, I do. Had the misfortune to be in school with him. Worst bully the alma mater ever produced, and that's going some."

"Abused you, did he?" There was awe in the green one's eyes as he assessed Mr. Clarence Smythe's size. "Still, I expect you were small once, actually."

"Not really," the other replied blandly. "Always big for me age, as a matter of fact. So I wasn't picked on. It was the little boys that suffered. The thing was, in school you expect a certain amount of bullying as a matter of course. Tradition. That sort of thing. But Monk was mean along with it. A nasty piece of work. At least back then. Still," he added doubtfully, "a cove can change."

Lord Crews chuckled, leaning confidentially across the table and lowering his voice to a mere whisper. "I doubt his disposition has improved of late. Have you heard what happened?"

Three heads shook.

"Well—" Crews glanced back over his shoulder to ascertain that Lord Monkhouse, his back turned toward them, had joined the play. "He was left at the church, as it were."

"You mean he was jilted?" The young one's eyes were wide.

"In the worst possible way. The wedding took place, actually. But when they got ready to leave the church, the bride was nowhere to be seen. The place was in an uproar. Friend of mine was there and told me of it. They searched St. Clement's from the undercroft to the steeple, but there was never a sign of her. They put it out, of course, that the bride had been kidnapped. But it's my friend's opinion that she scampered."

"Can't say as I blame her. Nasty piece of goods, that Monk," the giant repeated.

The conversation had Lord Jeremy's rapt attention. For some unknown reason his thumbs began to prick. "Who was she?" he asked Crews.

"Can't recall the name just now, but you wouldn't know her. Lived abroad. Her guardian's some kind of diplomat. The thing is, she's an heiress. Huge fortune, so my friend says. And a beauty. Rare combination. Stands to reason Monk would be up in the boughs. Got the hue and cry out, of course, but it's been about a month now with no sign of her."

"Hmmm," the giant mused. "Small wonder he looks like a volcano just ready to erupt. Monk needs an heiress the worst way. They say he's so far up River Tick that the cent-per-centers are about to close in on his estate."

"Shush!" Crews warned, frowning intently at his cards and playing one with a flourish out of turn.

Lord Monkhouse, seeming to sense he was the topic of conversation, was glaring their way. The whist game continued furiously and silently for several minutes under this scowling scrutiny till Lord Jeremy abruptly excused himself, called for his hat and stick, and went striding from the game room while his friends gaped after him.

He was up early the next morning and on his way to Grosvenor Street. As he strode along, he tried to manufacture an adequate excuse to offer his aunt for violating the prescribed hours for morning calls. None was forthcoming. For now, in the cold light of day, his suspicions of the evening before seemed absurd.

As it proved, he had no need to make excuses. "Her ladyship is not at home," Moffatt dolefully informed him.

"Up early, too, then, was she? Must have something to do with the moon's phase. Well, I'll just come in and wait till she gets back from her errand."

"I fear I did not make myself quite clear, sir. I should have said that her ladyship is away from home."

"Indeed?" Jeremy looked startled. "Out of town, you're saying?"

"I would assume so, sir." Moffatt was at his starchiest.

"What do you mean, you would assume so?"

"Her ladyship did not see fit to confide in me, sir. At her departure yesterday she simply stated that she planned to be away for an indefinite length of time."

At this point Lord Jeremy decided that the conversation should not continue on the doorstep. He preceded the butler inside.

"Now, what is the aunt up to, Moffatt?" he asked as soon as the door had closed behind them.

Though eager to cooperate, the butler was not a fount of information. He was able to tell his mistress's nephew only that she and her two friends had formed a club that apparently had to do with seeking out new experiences. "They plan to widen their horizons, so her ladyship told me. But when I inquired as to where this might take them," Moffatt sniffed, "she said that she planned to leave that up to providence."

"Good God!"

"Exactly, sir."

"Did she give the coachman any advance notice of her destination?"

"She did not take her traveling carriage, sir. The two of them left our premises in a hackney."

"You don't suppose she's planning to hole up here in London, do you? Perhaps she's with one or the other of my adopted aunts. Though why she would not have said so—"

"I took the liberty of checking Mrs. Abingdon's and Mrs. Oliver's residences, sir. And they, too, are gone. And without leaving their direction with their household staffs."

"This is all deuced odd."

"Exactly, sir. There is one thing, though—"

"Yes, Moffatt?"

"From something that Miss Adelaide let slip, her major domo thinks that they plan to go by public coach."

"Good God!"

"Yes, sir."

"And you've really no notion of what they're up to, Moffatt?" Lord Jeremy grinned suddenly. "The public coach! I can actually imagine Aunt Lavinia traveling in a public conveyance, but not Mary. Her consequence will never survive the comedown."

"Oh, but Mary did not accompany her ladyship."

"But you did say the *two* of them left here."

"She has taken Ki—er, the young person, sir."

"The new upstairs maid?" Lord Jeremy's thumbs were pricking once again.

Moffatt's attempt to keep his face impassive was not successful. "I refer to the person who came here as the upstairs maid, sir. Since you were last here, she has been through two transformations. First her ladyship made Kitty her personal maid. An assistant to Mary, she termed it. You can well imagine what Mary thought of that after forty years of devoted service."

Lord Jeremy could indeed.

"And when that arrangement did not work out satisfactorily, her ladyship then informed me that the young woman was actually her own cousin's child who for reasons of her own preferred to remain incognito."

"My God."

"Exactly, sir."

"Did she say *what* cousin?"

"No, sir."

"Dashed if I can think of one that fits the bill."

"Nor can I, sir."

"Still, when it comes to family, one does not bother to keep abreast."

"I suppose not, sir."

"One could have all sorts of unknown relations, I collect."

"If you say so, sir."

"Well—" Lord Jeremy's sigh was long-drawn-out and heartfelt. "I collect I shall have to try and discover what the old dragon is up to."

"I was hoping you would do so, m'lord."

"And I expect that the way to start is to visit the various posting houses and see if anyone remembers seeing our four ladies."

"Oh, I daresay they will be remembered, sir."

"Yes, my aunt does have a way of making her presence known, doesn't she?"

"Indeed. And if I may say so, sir, she has outdone herself this time."

Moffatt then went on to describe the outfits that Lady Lavinia and "Miss Pickering" had been wearing.

"Good God!" Lord Jeremy re-uttered. But faintly this time.

"Exactly, sir."

Moffatt's prediction proved correct. The White Horse Cellar was Lord Jeremy's second port of call. Any number of witnesses were able to report seeing the oddly dressed ladies and their two companions and to say with certainty that the quartet departed on the coach to Bath.

Lord Jeremy hurried back to his own rooms, where he ordered his valet to pack his things. He would leave immediately for an indefinite stay.

Chapter
Eight

"THIS MAKES ABSOLUTELY NO SENSE. NONE OF IT. What do you suppose she is up to?"

Jane gave her questioner an exasperated look as she sat propped up in bed, sipping her tea. Addie, still in her nightgown and cap, had arrived in her bedchamber along with the morning tray. Though normally of an amiable disposition, Jane did like to fortify herself with a cup of strongly brewed beverage prior to facing a fellow human being. And being forced to try to explore the complexities of Lady Lavinia Pickering's mind was, in her opinion, no way to start the day. She said so. "For heaven's sake, Addie, when have we ever known what Lavinia was up to? Just be thankful for small mercies, I say."

"But it does not make sense." As she drew up a chair, Addie stuck stubbornly to her theme. "That all that talk of 'enlarging our horizons' should land us in Bath is queer enough. But after riding on the public coach and seeing those outlandish outfits, I fully expected Lavinia to pitch wigwams for us on the Parade. Now, confess, Jane, did you not fear it?"

"Well," Jane mused, "fortunately 'wigwams' never occurred to me, but I certainly never expected anything so tamely conventional as a furnished house on the Royal Crescent that comes completely staffed." She looked around with approval at the charmingly furnished bedchamber, with its pale-yellow-silk–covered walls and matching window and bed curtains that reflected the tasteful decor of the rest of the house. It had been let to Lady Lavinia by a well-to-do gentleman now traveling upon the Continent. "But one must never look a gift horse in the mouth, Addie."

"Rubbish. This is not like her. And what do you make of the fact that she sent for the town's leading modiste the moment that we arrived? Lavinia Pickering never cares a fig about what she wears and you know it."

"Well, if I didn't know it before, I certainly do now." Jane closed her eyes and shuddered. "The sight of her clambering to the coach top in those appalling trousers will haunt me till my dying day. But as for the dressmaker"—she opened her eyes and continued practically—"that is easily explained. Catherine cannot be expected to make do with the one suitable outfit she owned when Lavinia employed her. And since she has to have a wardrobe, Lavinia would not be so churlish as to deny us the same privilege. Heaven knows we complained enough about just fourteen pounds of luggage."

"Well, I expect you are right," Addie conceded. "But now, Miss Logic and Reason, let's hear you explain Catherine. For if she is Lavinia's relation, well then, I'm his majesty's sister."

"God forbid," Jane murmured as she mentally reviewed that unattractive group.

"I have racked my brain over our family tree and I can come up with no one who has gone abroad to live."

"Possibly you have overlooked some adventurer."

"Fustian. The Pickerings are as provincial as they come. Lavinia is an aberration. The rest of her family, with the possible exception of Jeremy, are dull as can be. I tell you, that girl is no relation. And what is more," Addie declared, "I think she is at the bottom of this entire business. I believe that the whole club thing is just so much dust in our eyes. I believe that Lavinia's real purpose was to get that young woman out of London. Well, Jane, what do you say to that?"

But Jane was, for the moment, bereft of speech. It was entirely unlike Addie to have exerted her brain to this extent, and the fact that she had voiced Jane's own suspicions was a bit unnerving. "Well, you may be right," she finally managed to say. "But all the same, let us simply be thankful that things are progressing along so smooth a path."

"Yes, but for how long?" Addie asked darkly.

"Who knows. But the biblical 'sufficient unto the day is the evil thereof,' might well have been spoken with Lavinia Pickering in mind. So let us take no thought for the morrow."

"It is easy enough to preach while you are lying in bed, swilling tea, but—" Addie broke off as an elderly chambermaid, spruce in a pristine apron and mobcap, entered to announce that a "person" sent by the modiste was asking to see Mrs. Oliver. Mrs. Oliver's reaction was to turn beet-red.

"What is it, Addie?" Jane inquired curiously.

"Oh, nothing. Nothing at all." But she failed to meet her friend's eyes as she rose hastily to her feet. "Just a slight alteration to one of my gowns, that's all," she was saying as she hurried from the room.

Jane stared at the closed door for several seconds before pouring the last dregs of the tea into her Wedgwood cup. "That is the last, final, camel-breaking straw," she muttered as she sipped it. "If Addie, too, has turned mysterious, I vow that I shall scream."

"The four of us shall visit the Pump Room," Lady Lavinia announced after they had breakfasted, a rather strained meal since Jane and Adelaide were having difficulty adjusting to Catherine's sudden rise from servant to equal. It did not help that Catherine's replies to their awkward attempts at conversation were usually a simple yes or no. This time, though, she was more forthcoming. "May I please be excused, Lady Lavinia? I fear I am developing the headache."

"Oh, really?" Her ladyship's eyes lighted up. "How fortunate. No, I am sorry, Catherine, but it is most essential that you accompany us. For the Pickering Club's first scientific experiment will be to put the famous waters to the test. I should not say so, for the true scientist should retain an open mind, but I have always held strong reservations concerning the healing properties of these springs. Now, this is a famous turn of events. Your having the headache, I mean, Catherine. For the three of us are in such excellent health that we cannot put the efficacy of the waters to a true test."

"Humph!"

"Yes, Adelaide?"

"Excellent health, my eyebrow! Just because *you* never have an ache or pain. How like you to dismiss my weak chest."

"Well, ah, yes, of course that, too, will become a goal of our experimentation. But whereas it will take several weeks before we can gauge the results of the waters upon your chest, we shall be in a position to observe the immediate effects upon Catherine's headache."

"But—" Jane began, and then had second thoughts.

"You were about to say?"

She had been about to say that since Catherine's headache was obviously spurious, any serious experimentation was nullified. But she realized in time that that was hardly tactful. "You will be taking notes, I collect?" she substituted.

"A very good question. I suggest that we all carry our notebooks along and jot down our impressions. Then at our next meeting we can compare our findings and you shall put them in the proper form."

"Me? Why me?"

"Because," Lady Lavinia spoke patiently, "you are our secretary."

"I am the *corresponding* secretary. By the bye, with whom do you expect me to correspond? Moffatt, perhaps?"

"As I have pointed out before," Lavinia snapped, "sarcasm does not become you, Jane. But we are wasting time. The important thing is that we all become keen observers of our new surroundings. Now then, shall we change for our walk to the Pump Room and reconvene in a half hour's time?"

"Oh, dear!" An appalling thought struck Addie. "Lavinia, you are not going to wear those dreadful trousers, are you? For if so, I will tell you right now that I will not step one foot outside this house."

Catherine, too, looked apprehensive.

"Do not be absurd. There is no practical reason to do so in this instance. Except, perhaps"—a thoughtful look crept upon her countenance—"as an example of freedom to others of our sex. We Pickerings could, in the words of Henry the Fifth, become 'makers of manners.' "

"No, Lavinia," Jane said firmly.

"Oh, very well, then." Their leader rose to her feet. "In half an hour's time, then. We shall gather in the hall."

Chapter Nine

THE QUARTET ARRIVED AT THE PUMP ROOM, BREATH-less but respectably clad. "I hope these waters live up to their reputation," Jane commented, "for we shall need all our strength to reclimb that hill."

"The laws of gravity will certainly be against us in that direction," Catherine agreed in one of her very few unsolicited remarks.

The group paused inside the entryway and looked around them. The large saloon was pleasing to the eye, ornamented with Corinthian pillars and a handsome Tompion clock. A statue of Beau Nash, Bath's famous eighteenth-century master of ceremonies, gazed down benignly upon them from an elevated niche. The focal point of the Pump Room was, of course, a large bar dominated by an enormous marble vase.

The ladies were making their way toward it

when their progress was interrupted by a gentleman of the same generation as their majority. He beamed upon them. Indeed, it was difficult to decide the source of the greatest radiance: his smile, his coat (a vivid blue with highly polished silver buttons), his several gold rings, his dangling gold eyeglass, or the gold knob that topped his gleaming ebony cane. He was preceded by an aura of bouquet du roi that sent Addie into a sneezing fit and caused Jane to unobtrusively, she hoped, hold a handkerchief to her nose.

"You must be the Pickering party," the gentleman gushed. "And you are Lady Lavinia?" With obvious self-congratulation for his acumen, he singled out their leader.

Lavinia inclined her head stiffly, for once unsure whether to give the forward gentleman a set-down or not. Still, "when in Rome," and so on. Perhaps in Bath one did not stand on points.

The gentleman sensed her reserve and hastened to identify himself. His smile dimmed a bit in the process, however, for he was accustomed to instant recognition. "I have the honor to be master of ceremonies here," he informed them. "Allow me to welcome you to Bath, ladies, and entreat you to sign our book."

The occupants of the crowded room, appearing in some need of fresh diversion, gazed curiously as he led them to the register, where Lavinia recorded all of their names. As she did so, she was conscious of Catherine's gaze across her shoulder reading the most recent signatures. She felt—or imagined—a sense of relief on that young lady's part.

The ritual of registration completed, the master of ceremonies escorted them to the pump, recounting as he did so the wondrous cures effected throughout the years from the consumption of these miraculous waters. Lavinia hung upon his every word, and, to the gentleman's gratification, whipped out a small notebook from her reticule and jotted down the names and diseases and approximate dates of these cures.

After the gentleman had excused himself, she continued her research by quizzing the servant behind the bar. Her less scientific colleagues gazed curiously about them. The room was filled with middle-aged-and-over ladies and gentlemen. There were more of the former than the latter. Some were sipping from their quarter pints of water. Some were fortunate enough to have found seats, while some were promenading up and down, pretending that this was what they really wished to be doing.

"Jane," Addie called out, clutching her friend's arm, "don't look now, but we are being stared at."

"Obviously," the other murmured back. "But take no notice. What else is there to do in Bath?"

"No, you don't understand. We are being stared at in particular. It is the cigar-smoking gentleman from the coach."

"Indeed?" In spite of the injunction not to do so, Jane did look just in time to see the cigar smoker wave down the master of ceremonies and engage him in earnest conversation. At the conclusion of this brief interchange, the two gentlemen headed purposefully their way.

"Ladies"—the master of ceremonies reassumed his customary beam—"allow me to present Colonel Marston. Colonel Marston, it is my pleasure to make you known to Lady Lavinia Pickering, Miss Pickering, Mrs. Abingdon, and Mrs. Oliver."

"Actually, we are already acquainted," Jane frigidly reminded the colonel. "We rode down from London together, you may recall."

"Indeed I do," the colonel replied. "But I would never be so forward as to claim your acquaintance because of an intimacy you could not avoid. Nor did I, you may recall, presume to introduce myself under those forced circumstances."

"That was most thoughtful of you," Addie murmured, and received a look of approval from the gentleman. He now focused all of his attention upon her. "I was most eager, Mrs. Oliver, to inquire of your health. I trust you have recovered from the rigors of our coach ride?"

"Oh, yes, indeed, sir." She blushed. "Thank you for your concern."

"Mrs. Oliver has been ill, has she?" The master of ceremonies rubbed his hands together, not quite, but almost in glee. "Well then, madam, you must not delay your course of the waters. I can assure you you will be right as rain in no time. Their efficacy is renowned."

Jane was about to make a remark concerning the efficacy of an absence of cigar smoke, but a glance at the colonel's concerned face made her conclude that such a remark would be mean-spirited.

"And, er, will Mr. Oliver be joining you, ma'am?" he was asking rather awkwardly.

"Oh, dear me, no." Addie looked flustered. "Mr. Oliver—Lieutenant Oliver, that is—left us many years ago."

"What my cousin means to say is that he died." Lady Lavinia disliked euphemisms.

"Oh, I say, I am sorry." The colonel, however, did not look it.

"A military man, you say?" The words were addressed to Mrs. Oliver.

"Why, yes. My late husband served in the Fifty-second Regiment of Foot."

"Did he, by Jove! You don't mean to say! My word! This is a coincidence. That is my old regiment."

"How very extraordinary!" Adelaide was staring at the colonel as if some sort of miracle had taken place.

"Extraordinary?" Lavinia mused. "Is that not overstating the matter? Given the number of men required to constitute a regiment, I should think that the chances of coming across one of them were quite high indeed."

Either Colonel Marston did not hear her or else he was uninterested in the laws of probability. His eyes were darting all around the room. They suddenly lighted up. "Oh, I say. Those people are just leaving. Allow me to commandeer their table while you ladies fill your tumblers." Without waiting for permission, he dashed off to complete his part of the mission.

"Well, of all the presumption. How dare he assume—" Lavinia glared.

"Oh, but I think he meant no presumption." Addie was looking quite distressed by her cousin's attitude. "Tables are extremely scarce. And by the time he delayed to do the proper, someone else would have taken it."

"And all to the good. We shall walk about as we drink our waters."

Jane studied Addie's crestfallen expression. And though she had no more desire for the colonel's company than had Lavinia, she felt moved to protest. "Aren't you forgetting the objectives of the Pickering Club, Lavinia? Surely this comes under the heading of new experiences. It is not at all like you to stand on ceremony."

"And he may have known my dear Lieutenant Oliver," Addie pleaded.

"I must confess I should like very much to sit awhile," the youngest member, who had also noted Addie's reaction, chimed in to everyone's surprise. "I am exhausted."

"Oh, very well, then." Lavinia capitulated with a modicum of grace and turned toward the marble bar.

Jane gave her tumbler of the famous waters a suspicious look. The yellowish cast, she noted, was decidedly off-putting. "I do wish I had observed whether these glasses were clean before they were filled," she muttered as they threaded their way, single file, through the crowd toward the table that the colonel fiercely guarded.

"Surely this, too, comes under the heading of new experiences?" Lavinia gleefully hurled Jane's own words back in her teeth.

"And if it were not nasty," Catherine laughed, "it could not be good for us." The young woman seemed to be blooming in these new surroundings, à la the Pickering Club philosophy.

"Ah, ladies." The colonel scampered around the table, pulling out chairs. "This is, indeed, an honor."

Even Lavinia looked a bit mollified by so much deference.

There was a momentary silence while the Pickering Club, as one, took experimental sips of the mineral waters. As one, they wrinkled up their noses and shuddered.

"How vile!" was Jane's comment.

"Oh, yes, but most salubrious," the colonel said encouragingly. "I have been coming here yearly since I went on half pay, and I can assure you that I am in the pink of health."

"Yes, but can you be certain that the waters get the credit?" Lavinia asked with interest.

"Not a doubt in my mind, dear lady."

"Hmmm." Lavinia made an entry in her notebook.

The colonel looked down at Addie, whom he had seated beside him. "I have been trying to place your late husband, ma'am. Was sure I knew him. And now I have it. Tall cove, wasn't he? With ginger hair. A bit of a stoop."

"Well, no. As a matter of fact, Lieutenant Oliver had fair hair and was slightly less than average in height."

The colonel snapped his fingers then and beamed. "Of course. I have it now. The very fellow. Died a hero's death at Quatre Bras."

"Actually," Lady Lavinia corrected him dryly, "Lieutenant Oliver died of the grippe at Aldershot."

The colonel shifted his gaze from Addie to Lavinia. "Losing one's life while in the service of one's country is a hero's death, ma'am."

Lavinia had the grace to look abashed. "I stand corrected," she said with what passed, in her case, for humility.

"Tell me, Colonel Marston"—Jane tactfully switched the subject as she observed Addie's eyes beginning to mist—"what does one do in Bath?"

"Oh, I can assure you that your time will be so

filled, you will wonder where it went. One must take the waters twice a day, of course. And to get their maximum effect, this should be followed by a constitutional."

"Just getting ourselves back to the Crescent will take care of that," Jane sighed.

"And of course there are the reading rooms. And the theater. And, by Jove, tomorrow is Wednesday. Oh, I say, what luck!"

"And what is so significant about Wednesday?" Lavinia asked.

"Why, it is a ball night, ma'am. You ladies must not miss it. I can assure you that the Assembly Rooms are of the utmost elegance. And as for the company—well, ladies, you will find nothing in the society there to disgust you. Goes without saying that no tradespeople are admitted. You will like it above half, I can assure you."

Catherine, Jane noted, was beginning to show signs of anxiety. Addie's eyes, on the other hand, sparkled with pleasure. Lavinia appeared to be turning the matter over in her head.

The colonel pushed his advantage. "Pray, allow me, madam, the pleasure of securing tickets for your party."

Lady Lavinia's head snapped up. The look she gave the colonel was one that no subaltern would have dared. "I can assure you, Colonel Marston, that we require no assistance. We are capable of making our own arrangements."

Chapter Ten

L ADY LAVINIA DID NOT LIKE TO BE KEPT WAITING.
"Oh, do sit down." Jane looked up from her needlework. "Your pacing is making me dizzy. And what precisely is the point? I cannot believe that you, of all people, are so eager to attend an assembly."

"Of course I am not eager. I am, in point of fact, quite resigned to being bored to distraction. But there is a principle at stake. If a thing is supposed to begin at a certain time, then that is the time to be there."

"Nonsense. It is quite unfashionable to be on time. Shows a lack— Ah, here are the truants now."

Jane was only partly right. Catherine hurried into the withdrawing room, where her elders sat, an apology already forming on her lips. "Oh, I am sorry to have kept you waiting. My new gown had to be rehemmed at the last moment. Eliza thought it too long for dancing, and even though I assured her I would not be taking the floor, she insisted. Is Mrs. Oliver not here yet? I must confess I am relieved."

Lady Lavinia was surveying her charge closely with a proprietary kind of satisfaction. She nodded approvingly. "You look very nice, m'dear."

Jane found the remark a gross understatement. She was of the opinion that Catherine looked stunning. Her dress was of white tulle over a white satin slip and ornamented with Provins roses. She had fashioned a makeshift toque from a length of net, which was wound about her head.

"But I do not think you will need that headdress," Lavinia frowned. "The weather is quite pleasant. And it is a shame to hide your lovely hair."

For some unaccountable reason, Catherine's face grew rosy. But at that moment the older ladies' attention was distracted by the breathless entrance of their contemporary.

"Well, I must say it is about time," Lady Lavinia lectured. "It is most inconsiderate, Adelaide, to keep others—" She broke off suddenly, her face appalled. "My God! What have you done to yourself?"

Addie's face now outglowed Catherine's. "I am sure I don't know what you mean," she countered.

It took Jane longer to notice what it was that had sent Lavinia into such a taking. At first glance Addie looked unusually nice. Her gray Turkish satin gown was quite becoming. It was only after Jane's eyes had scanned up and down her friend's figure twice that the new contour registered. She gasped aloud. Then, with difficulty, smothered a giggle.

"You know perfectly well what I mean," Lavinia was saying. "I am referring to your bosom."

Addie went a few shades pinker.

"What about my bosom?" she managed to say.

"You now have one."

"Well, I certainly feel that this conversation is highly indelicate. No one but you, Lavinia, would remark upon such a thing. It does you little credit."

"Indeed? And if you suddenly grew a third eye in the middle of your forehead, I collect I should not remark upon that either?"

"Wh-what have you done, Addie dear." Jane struggled for composure.

"If you must know," the other replied haughtily, "I am wearing a bust improver."

"One of those awful wax contraptions?" Lavinia shook her head in disbelief. "I thought they went out of fashion eons ago. And good riddance to them. Go take the thing off. Why anyone in her right mind would wish to protrude in such a bizarre fashion is beyond me."

"That's easy enough for you to say," Addie replied huffily, looking pointedly at her cousin's ample frontage. "Besides, what happened to the Pickering determination to try new things? And I will have you know that I am wearing this at the modiste's insistence. She said that this new fashion with the lowered waist and fuller skirt-line needs more, er, bulk at the top. For balance, as it were."

"Humph!" Lavinia snorted.

"I think it looks very nice, Mrs. Oliver." After a successful struggle to keep her face straight, Catherine did her best to pour oil on the troubled waters.

Addie gave her a grateful look. Then it was her turn to look astounded. "My goodness, Catherine, what have you done to your hair?"

Lavinia and Jane refocused their attention. While all eyes had been fixed upon Addie, Catherine's scarf had shifted just enough to reveal the soft curls clustered on her forehead. They had been transformed from their natural flaxen hue to a duller medium brown.

"I used a walnut dye," Catherine replied defensively, removing the scarf. "I've always wondered what it would be like to be brunette. So, like Mrs. Oliver, I thought it quite in the spirit of the Pickering Club to try an experiment. Does it look so horrible?"

"Oh, no. No, indeed," Jane said hastily. "It looks quite nice, in fact. It's just that your natural color is so lovely that I cannot see why you would wish—"

"Never mind, Jane," Lavinia interrupted firmly. "Catherine, and, for that matter, Adelaide, has the right to alter her appearance in any way she chooses. So unless you, too, have some startling transfiguration to reveal, I suggest that we go."

Despite Jane's protest, Lavinia had insisted that they walk. She led them at a rapid clip down Brock Street and around the Circus. They arrived, breathless, at the Assembly Rooms on the stroke of eight and threaded their way through the fleet of sedan chairs disembarking their passengers at the entrance.

Bath was full of company. And that company, with little else to do, choked the building's corridor, obstructed the octagonal antechamber and then redistributed itself to merely crowd the ballroom on the left and the tearoom on the right with sufficient patrons left over to fill the long card room addition.

The master of ceremonies, wearing his usual fixed smile, was busily greeting the company. As he bowed low to Lady Lavinia, Colonel Marston, who had been hovering behind him, swooped down upon Adelaide.

"Ah, Mrs. Oliver, here you are at last. I have been hoping to have the honor of partnering you at cards."

"Oh, indeed?" Addie had turned a becoming pink and looked toward her cousin as if seeking permission.

"Go with them, Jane," Lavinia commanded, much to that lady's disgust. She wondered whether she was being delegated as a chaperon for Addie or as an ally. Their friend's abysmal card-playing certainly needed all the assistance possible.

"I shall accompany Catherine to the ballroom," Lavinia continued. "That would bore you to distraction, I am sure."

Jane gave her a speaking glare. She had quite looked forward to watching the dancing and could imagine nothing more tedious than an evening spent in the colonel's company. Still, this did not seem the proper place for a rebellion. Colonel Marston put a protective hand under Addie's elbow. Jane trailed, martyrlike, behind.

"Really, Lady Lavinia," Catherine murmured after they had entered the enormous ballroom which was thronged with people and ablaze with the light from a row of candelabra that marched down the center of the ceiling plasterwork, "I do not care to dance."

Lavinia had neither failed to note how her young companion's eyes had anxiously swept the room, nor the fact that there had been no jolt of recognition on her part. "Nonsense," she said. "There is no reason why you should not. You have attended balls before?"

"Yes, certainly."

"And did you lack for partners?"

"Why, no."

"I thought not." Lady Lavinia was looking thoughtfully at her young friend's hair. "Do you happen to recall just what percentage of the dances you stood up for?"

"Well, usually all of them."

"I see. That should make comparison quite simple."

"I beg pardon, Lady Lavinia, but I am not sure that I understand."

"Simple. Whereas I feel the need to point out that both you and Adelaide have sadly perverted the goals of the Pickering Club by applying its principles to such trivialities as personal appearance, still, what is done is done. And it does give one a golden opportunity for applying the scientific method. Thank goodness, I did put my notebook inside my reticule. We shall endeavor to discover tonight just what effect a change of hair coloration has upon a young lady's social life."

"I see." A smile twitched at Catherine's lips. "Does it make a difference that I had many acquaintances among the gentlemen at those other balls, whereas here I am a stranger?"

"Hmmm. I shall certainly make a note to that effect. We shall see what develops."

She spied two empty chairs among those encircling the walls and was headed toward them with Catherine in tow, when the master of ceremonies waylaid them. "Ah, Lady Lavinia, may I present Mr. Blakeney of Blakeney Hall? He is most desirous of dancing the cotillion with your young cousin."

As the couple took the floor, Lady Lavinia made her way alone to the empty chairs. Once settled, she drew out her notebook, wrote in a heading, and recorded the number one.

Chapter
Eleven

THE COLONEL QUICKLY COMMANDEERED THE LAST CARD
table. Unfortunately, a very formidable lady of
ancient years and forbidding expression was en-
sconced there. She proved to be a Mrs. Thane-Wilson,
widow of a long-departed general whose consequence
she was determined to keep alive. "Cut" was her
one-word acknowledgment of their introduction.

All in all, Jane reflected with the resignation of an
early Christian martyr, it was a very good thing that
it fell her lot to partner the dowager. For she quickly
deduced that this longtime resident of Bath had been
studiously avoided by the other players. The general's
wife would doubtlessly tear Addie to pieces.

But it soon became apparent that where partners
were concerned, it was a case of the devil and the
deep blue sea. The colonel and the distaff general
proved to be old foes of the card table, each out for

the other's blood and each prone to take his or her partner to task for any mishap in play.

Being a superior player did not save Jane from criticism. But the fact that she was unruffled by any post-mortem demands of why she had not "finessed the heart" or "led through the honor" took some of the wind out of the widow's sails. She therefore turned on Addie, the more natural victim.

This seemed unsporting to say the very least, for that unfortunate lady had quickly incurred the displeasure of her own partner. After receiving a severe lecture from the colonel for playing the wrong card entirely, Addie began studying her hand intently at each turn, trying to avoid a similar mistake. This tactic had no noticeable effect upon the quality of her game; it did, however, incur the wrath of Mrs. Thane-Wilson for "taking all night to play one card." Jane longed to kick her partner when she rattled poor Addie into leading to her ace of diamonds. She retaliated instead by playing her trey and losing the trick. She then smiled sweetly as the old lady glared.

The colonel, at least, was mollified. But only for a moment. Addie was then forced to play a hand; she went down abysmally. This provoked a lecture upon strategies unperceived.

Jane was ready to rescue her friend and flee the table, but she was not quick enough. Mrs. Thane-Wilson's predatory talons had swooped down upon the pack and begun to deal.

Perspiration gleamed upon Addie's forehead. A glazed look came into her eyes. She played her cards like a somnambulist. Each ill-chosen selection was followed by a reproachful sigh from the colonel and a snort of derision from the dowager.

Jane began to bend all her considerable skills toward losing the rubber as quickly as possible. But her efforts were offset by Addie's blunders and the dowager's propensity for cheating. The colonel seemed aware of Mrs. Thane-Wilson's style of play but, due perhaps to some military code, neglected to call her on it.

Jane listened with envy to the high-spirited chatter all around them, marveling that card games could actually be fun instead of torture. She avoided looking at her friend, finding her agonized expression too painful to witness. Then some movement from the table behind Addie caused her to glance that way. Jane's eyes bugged out with horror.

Addie, her face contorted by concentration as she peered glassily at her cards, squirmed in her chair. Her hand descended and retreated while she strove to make a choice. And as she writhed with indecision, her bosom appeared to be doing its own counterdance. She squirmed to the right. It shifted left. She reversed herself. It did the same. And all the while it drifted slowly, inexorably, down toward her midriff, like a pair of ducks flying lower and lower, back and forth, before finally settling upon the water.

Any hope Jane had that this physical anomaly was unnoticed died aborning. The colonel, mouth agape, stared in fascinated horror. The dowager removed her circular spectacles, polished them in disbelief, replaced them upon her nose, and leaned across the table. Her magnified myopic eyes moved in synchronization with the bust enhancer.

Jane had prudently brought along a shawl for the walk back home. She now snatched it from her chair post and draped it around Addie's shoulders. "You are in a draft, dear," she murmured. "I fear you will catch a chill."

"Are you daft?" Addie said crossly. "It is hot as anything in here. I vow, the candles might as well be bonfires." And she impatiently shrugged off the shawl.

But in the act of doing so, her eyes fell upon her fallen figure, nestling below her rib cage, impeded in its downward progress by the ribbon that encircled her evening gown. Addie gave Jane a piteous, heart-rending look, and swooned.

Lord Jeremy had had a busy day. He had made the trip from London to Bath in record time. He had obtained a room at the White Hart. He had discovered his aunt's direction, only to learn when he called at the Royal Crescent that the ladies were attending the assembly. He had been summarily prevented from entering those hallowed rooms by reason of improper dress. He had rushed back to his hotel and changed into his black satin tailcoat and white satin smalls. He now stood in the musician's gallery (glared at by the violinist whose elbow he was hampering), gazing down into the ballroom.

He had no difficulty in locating his aunt. She sat alone, watching the cotillion with interest. There was a notebook on her lap. She occasionally scribbled some jottings into it.

But Jeremy failed to find the main object of his quest. He systematically scanned the dancers for a third time, looking for that particular head of golden hair. He was just turning away to search the card room, when a glimpse of a face tilted upward to listen to some remark from a tall partner caused him to freeze and then lean over the railing for a perilous look.

"I'll be damned," he muttered to himself as he

turned away, then hurried along the balcony and down the grand staircase. He was just in time, as the set broke up, to insinuate himself between Miss Pickering and a waiting partner. "Ah, cousin," he beamed. "Well met, indeed. Here I was, thinking I did not know a soul in Bath and I spy you in the crowd. This is famous. By Jove, it really is.

"Oh, I say, sir"—he turned the full force of his charm on the glowering gentleman at his elbow—"is this your dance? Pray do forgive me, but my cousin and I haven't seen each other for donkey's years and we've a lot of catching up to do." Before the would-be partner—or Catherine, for that matter—could protest, he led her onto the floor.

Lord Jeremy was both a kind man and, he feared, a smitten man. The fact that the young lady with him had gone deathly pale at his appearance was most unnerving. "Oh, I say," he murmured as they threaded through the crush, "no need to look like that. I'm not about to interfere in whatever you and my old horror of an aunt are up to. We do need to talk, though. Didn't I see a tearoom around here somewhere? Might as well get our sixpence worth, don't you think?"

He found two empty places near the double tier of Corinthian columns that adorned the tearoom and led Catherine to them. "Don't run away now; I'll be right back." True to his word, he soon returned, balancing two cups. "As a restorative, this may leave a bit to be desired," he observed as he handed her one. "I expect that these leaves were first used by the Romans. The water's barely colored."

Even so, Catherine sipped the brew gratefully. Jeremy sat beside her and studied her profile thoughtfully.

"Must you stare so?"

"Oh, was I staring? I do beg pardon. Quite rag-mannered, of course. But it does come as a bit of a shock, you know. Not that it isn't attractive. Though to be quite honest, I do prefer your natural shade. Oh, Lord, have I put my foot in my mouth? Perhaps this is your natural shade."

She didn't deign to reply, so he filled the silence. "Well, never mind. It occurs to me now that maybe nature has nothing to say to either color. You probably have a new one for each metamorphosis. Though perhaps I should not do so, may I offer a word of criticism? I think your present color would have done best for upstairs maid and the golden stuff seems more suited to your present status. Still, perhaps you know best. Did you go gray as an abigail?"

"Lord Jeremy"—she turned on him haughtily—"I thought you just said that you did not plan to interfere."

"Oh, I don't. Believe me. For I see my aunt Lavinia's fine Italian hand at work, and I know to my sorrow that trying to interfere with her is like trying to stop a tidal wave. But I did not say that I wasn't curious. One minute a maid. The next a relation. It does cause one furiously to think."

"An exercise you are unaccustomed to?"

"Now, that was low. No need to be offensive."

"I beg pardon, then. But your arrival here comes as a jolt. Just why are you following us?"

"Following you? Why ever would I do a thing like that?"

"That was my question. Don't tell me that a Bond Street beau like yourself has come here for a course of the waters."

"Why not? They are reported to cure almost anything."

"Including curiosity?"

"Well now, I was rather counting on you for that. Just how does it happen, Miss Pickering, that we are related?"

"You will have to ask your aunt, sir. I have never been quite able to sort out the Pickering family tree, but she seems to have no difficulty."

"No, she wouldn't."

"I do understand, however, that the relationship is quite remote."

"Well, that is a relief. Whereas cousins do marry all the time, I'm not much in favor of it. It seems to lead to all sorts of strange anomalies. Pointed heads. Sixth toes. Why, just look at our royal family."

Neither noticed Lady Lavinia's approach until she cleared her throat and they found her looming over them.

"Well, nephew, what brings you to Bath?"

He rose to his feet and bowed over her hand. "I'm here to visit an old school chum who is taking the waters on the advice of his quack. Has dropsy or some such thing. Bit of luck finding you ladies here. Last thing I would have expected."

"Humph!" The black eyes impaled him. He strove to remember that he was not five years old and need not squirm. "I have never decided, Jeremy, whether it is a character flaw or an admirable trait that you are an abominable liar.

"But come, Catherine, we must be going. I just received word that Adelaide has been taken suddenly ill. Good night, Jeremy. Good-bye, I should say. Do not for a moment consider staying on in tedious Bath merely for our sakes."

Chapter
Twelve

"I SHALL NEVER SHOW MY FACE IN BATH AGAIN," Addie wailed for the hundredth time while Jane struggled to retain her sympathy. She was finding it difficult to be patient. She had, after all, listened to Addie's hysterics in the sedan chair, supported her through Lavinia's inquisition, sat up with her half the night, and arrived back in her bedchamber with the early morning tea. Enough was enough.

"And I shall never play cards again." The jeremiad continued.

"Nonsense. You simply must remember not to squirm in your chair and cause your bust improver to come untied, that's all." Jane struggled not to laugh.

Addie thumped her teacup down on the bedside table and straightened her nightcap. "You surely don't think I will ever wear that infernal contraption again?" She glared at Jane, who was stretched out on a rosewood couch, sipping her tea. "I gave strict orders to the maid to throw it in the dustbin."

Jane's mind boggled at the possible reactions when the dustman found the thing. Would he think it a dismembered body at first glance?

"And I shall never play whist again, because I'm st-stupid."

"Fustian. You know you do quite well in congenial company," Jane prevaricated. "That obnoxious pair last night would have put even Lavinia off her game."

"Do you think so?" Addie's face brightened, then quickly fell. "No. In the first place, Lavinia would never t-trump her partner's ace. But even if she had, she could be depended upon to counter one of Mrs. Thane-Wilson's nasty remarks with a setdown of her own."

Jane could not deny the truth of that. There was a moment's silence while Addie replenished her tea from the silver pot. After a sip or two she said, trying unsuccessfully to sound casual, "You surely are not putting Colonel Marston in the same category with that odious Mrs. Thane-Wilson, are you?"

"He was just as prone as she to take exception to every card you played, was he not?"

"Well, gentlemen cannot help themselves when it comes to instructing us weaker vessels, can they? Besides, since he was my partner, he had the right. Whereas for Mrs. Thane-Wilson, well, Christian forbearance prevents me from saying more.

"No, I have sunk myself below redemption in the colonel's eyes. In the first place, my abysmal cardplay will have disgusted him, I am sure. But then,

when my false bosom slid down my dress front—
Jane, how dare you laugh! Oh, I shall never forget
his look of horror. I can never bear to look him in
the face again. And I know that he will be at great
pains to avoid me from now on."

With effort Jane refrained from saying "good riddance." Instead, "Are you going to remain in bed
all day?" she asked as she rose to her feet.

"I am going to remain in bed for the rest of my
life," her friend moaned tragically.

At that point the door opened and the maid's
mobcapped head poked through it. "There's a gentleman who's asking to see you, Mrs. Oliver."

"A gentleman?" Addie popped upright from her
pillow. "Who is it?"

"Colonel Marston, ma'am."

"Oh, dear! Oh, Jane! Oh, my goodness! I cannot
possibly face him. Oh, do tell him to go away. Tell
him I am unwell this morning."

"Her ladyship said as how you might say so,
mum," the maid replied with a solemn face. "And
she said that in case you did, I was to say that if
you ain't in the drawing room in fifteen minutes,
she was going to escort the gentleman to your bedchamber."

The time limit had two minutes yet to go when
Adelaide appeared, quavering, on the threshold of
the green and white striped withdrawing room.
Her arrival put an end to an awkward scene.
Lavinia and Colonel Marston had long since run
out of small talk. The colonel had pulled a cigar
from an inside pocket, been glared at by his hostess, and had put it back again. Since Lavinia ab-
horred needlework, the usual resource for idle

fingers, she drummed hers impatiently upon the octagonal table beside her chair instead. As Addie appeared, she leapt to her feet in relief. "Oh, there you are at last. I know the colonel will excuse me now. I have a rather important matter to attend to." She swept from the room with a Parthian shot. "I was unaware, you see, that calls were paid so early here in Bath."

Keeping his eyes carefully averted from the bosom area, the colonel looked anxiously at Addie's face. When she entered timidly and took a chair some distance from the one he had been occupying, he quickly crossed the room to sit beside her. A closer look at her tear-ravaged features was obviously unsettling.

"Oh, dear lady, I have hardly closed my eyes all night from worry. I fear I have scandalized your cousin by calling so early, but I could not wait until the proper hour to see how you were faring. Nor could I trust a messenger. I had to see for myself. Are you all right, Mrs. Oliver?"

"Y-yes." Her voice failed to carry conviction.

"I cannot begin to tell you how relieved I am to hear you say so. I don't mind admitting that when you swooned, it was one of the worst moments I have experienced in my entire life."

"It was?" Addie mustered the nerve to actually look at him through widened eyes. There was no mistaking the sincerity of his concern.

"I am afraid that I made a complete cake of myself, as the young people would say," she murmured.

"Nonsense!" he rebutted stoutly. "Fainting shows a ladylike sensibility, I always say. Besides," he hastened to add as her cheeks pinkened, "the place was unhealthily close. All those candles burning up the good air, don't you know. I'm only surprised that the entire female population did not swoon.

"But there was another little matter I was concerned about." He cleared his throat delicately and colored a bit himself. Addie braced herself, not knowing which way to look and wondering whether it would overdo ladylike sensibility to swoon again when he inquired about her peripatetic bosom. "I do hope you did not let that old behemoth's constant nagging distress you. Owe you an apology. Should never have let you in for such an evening. Can't stand to play with the old battle-ax myself, but I did not see any way to avoid it. Still, if I had known she would scold you all evening, I would have flatly refused to play. It was the outside of enough the way she went on and on at you. Had half a mind to tell her what was what."

"Oh, did you?" Addie gazed up at him gratefully. "Well, I am very glad that you did not. It would have not been at all the thing."

"No, I collect not," he sighed. "One must be the gentleman. Still, she had it coming."

"She is rather—overbearing. But then, she is an excellent card player. And I realize that I can be— rather trying. It is so difficult for me, you see, to keep all those cards straight in my head. I am sure that you also experienced a bit of Mrs. Thane-Wilson's disgust, since you yourself are a nonpareil."

"A nonpareil?" He reddened with pleasure and tried to appear modest. "No such thing," he expostulated. "The disgust business, I mean. You are a charming partner. And if I appeared to be, uh, instructing overzealously, it was only my attempt to

91

give that old walrus no reason to go on and on at you in that infernal way.

"Well now." He rose abruptly to his feet. "Mustn't outstay myself. Already committed a faux pas by calling so early. But can't tell you how relieved it has made me. You will be taking the waters, will you not, Mrs. Oliver? Best thing in the world for the swoons, they tell me."

"Well then, yes, I collect that I should."

"Famous! I shall see you, then, at the Pump Room. Till then, dear lady." He bent solicitously over her hand, then strode, in military fashion, from the room.

Adelaide, her cheeks still flushed, absently picked up a fan from the worktable and plied it back and forth as she stared at the now-empty doorway.

Chapter
Thirteen

LORD JEREMY WAS DEEP IN THOUGHT. HIS EYES WERE
cast down upon the pavement as he trudged
up Brock Street. He could not decide what approach to take in his hoped-for interview with his
aunt. Should he come at the subject obliquely in a
kind of "by the bye" fashion? Miss Addie's health,
he decided, could serve as an excuse for the early
call. From there he could casually move the conversation along without arousing suspicion as to
the real purpose of his visit. By Jove, it just might
work. His spirits rose, then plummeted as swiftly.
His aunt Lavinia would see through him like an
open window. He had never bamboozled her in his
entire life. No, perhaps the best approach
would—

"Look out, you fool!" an imperious voice rang out.
Lord Jeremy's head snapped up and his jaw

dropped. For a fatal moment he was frozen as an apparition rapidly approached.

And then Lord Jeremy jumped. The apparition swerved—wobbled—dipped—uprighted—rewobbled—careened into a wrought-iron fence. Lady Lavinia Pickering landed with a sickening thud upon the pavement.

"Oh, my God!"

Lord Jeremy dashed to his elderly relative's side. She lay, breathing heavily, sprawled out face downward on the gleaming granite squares. Her pantalooned legs were spread-eagled. Her tunic was bunched inelegantly underneath her armpits. Her palms still pressed the too-too-solid rock where they had tried to break her fall. "Oh, dear God! Are you all right? Aunt Livy, speak to me!"

"I would not advise that if I were you, Jeremy." The utterance forced its way between clenched teeth. "For I just might tell you what I think of fools who do not look where they are going. And do not call me Livy. I abhor Livy. Just because I tolerated it from a backward two-year-old who could not articulate Lavinia does not mean that I wish to hear it spewing from out a grown man's mouth. Stop that! What the devil do you think you are doing?"

What he was doing was running his hands up and down her limbs. "I am trying to discover if you've broken anything. And may I say that I consider profanity from the mouth of a gently bred female of, uh, mature years far less acceptable than a childish term of endearment from the lips of a grown man. Ah, now. Your arms and legs seem intact at least. Do you think you can sit up?"

"Of course I can sit up," she barked, and did so.

94

"Never mind about me. See to the hobby horse." She reached out and retrieved her tasseled cap from its upside down position and clapped it on her head. Jeremy gave her one more uneasy look. "I am not about to expire while your back is turned," she snapped. "Do as I ask you."

He went obediently to rescue the two-wheeled contraption from its resting place between the iron pickets of the fence. It wobbled ominously as he rolled it back to where Lavinia sat.

"Oh, dear." A look of consternation spread across her face. "Is it broken?"

"Yes, I fear we shall have to shoot the poor beast. The front wheel seems to be bent all out of shape."

"Your levity is entirely inappropriate, Jeremy. The hobby horse is not mine. It belongs to a lad who lives two houses from me in the Crescent. He kindly allowed me to borrow it. I wished to try the thing out before making my own purchase. And I will say that I was doing splendidly before you crossed my path.

"The trick is, you see, to propel the thing along by a kind of skipping motion of the feet until one gets up a certain speed. Then I discovered that if one holds one's limbs straight out in front, they interfere with the velocity to a lesser degree than when one merely allows them to dangle. There is a drawback to that position, however," she added grimly. "When one finds one's way obstructed by a moon-calf, wool-gathering ninnyhammer, there is not sufficient time to lower one's feet and drag the vehicle to a standstill." She began to struggle upright, resisting his attempts to help her.

"Well, tell me this. Just how did you avoid impaling yourself upon one of those iron fence spikes?"

He had tried to sound offhand, but shuddered nonetheless.

"I jumped, of course. A maneuver I could not have accomplished, may I point out, had I been wearing the customary hampering clothing that convention forces upon my sex."

"Well, yes, I can see that." Jeremy looked his aunt up and down, struggling not to smile. "I had heard your garments described by various witnesses, but the descriptions pale before the actuality."

"Humph." She was examining the hobby horse, feeling the leather saddle for stability and testing the handlebars. But whereas those parts of the machine seemed stable enough, there was no denying the fact that the front wheel was warped past all redemption. "Oh, dear." Jeremy did not recall ever having seen his aunt out of countenance before. "I do not know how I am going to be able to face that lad. He was rather reluctant, you see, to lend me his hobby horse."

Jeremy could well imagine but refrained from saying so. "I do not think there will be a problem," he ventured to suggest. "You will simply buy him the new one that you had intended purchasing. And if you are thinking, dear aunt, that you will have this one repaired and keep it for yourself, dismiss the thought. I intend to heave it off of Pulteney Bridge. And if you so much as look at a hobby horse in the future, I shall write your brother the earl to have you committed. Now then. Do you think you can walk?"

Although Jeremy offered to go inform the hobby-horse owner of the demise of his steed and make proper restitution, his aunt would have none of it.

"It goes against my principles to shirk my duty," she informed him haughtily. "I will deal with the consequences of my own actions, nephew."

Jeremy, therefore, entered the Crescent alone, prepared to wait for the interview with his aunt that he had insisted upon. He strolled into the library, his hands in his pockets, then pulled up short at the sight confronting him.

Miss Catherine Pickering was standing on the topmost rung of the movable ladder that provided access to the volumes on the highest shelves. She was on tiptoe, holding a large cloth in her right hand and was flailing away with it.

Jeremy ambled over to stand at the foot of the ladder and gaze up with interest at the maneuver for several seconds. "Dusting, are we?" he finally remarked. "Oh, no. My mistake. I now see that you are merely murdering flies."

Catherine emitted a startled shriek and tumbled backward. Jeremy caught her, and finding that fate had placed her in the very position of his most cherished fantasies, did not pause to analyze his luck. He kissed her.

After a breathless interlude that he found both satisfactory and devastating, Lord Jeremy set Catherine on her feet and prepared to employ the boxer's bob and weave that he had perfected in Cribb's parlor. (Not for a moment did he believe that she would employ the defensive technique recommended by his aunt.) But the anticipated slap was not forthcoming. He was pleased to note that she looked almost as shaken as he was.

With an obvious effort Catherine pulled herself together. "You should break yourself of the odious habit of sneaking up on people," she said crossly. "And of—that other thing as well."

He tried to look contrite. "I collect I should have cleared my throat or something in the doorway," he admitted. "But the truth is, I was too busy trying to figure out what you were doing. But as for the 'other thing,' I don't have a hope of reform there. I seem quite unable to help myself."

Catherine appeared to notice for the first time that she was twisting the cloth nervously in her hands, and with a second effort of will stopped it. "If you are looking for your aunt," she said formally, "I regret to say that she is out for the moment."

"Oh, I'm well aware of my aunt's whereabouts. It's you I'd like to talk to."

"We have nothing to discuss, Lord Jeremy." She tried to walk past him, but he blocked her way.

"Oh, yes, we do have." He looked earnestly into her eyes. "I was hoping you might realize that I am your friend."

She gave him a speaking look. "I have observed that your behavior toward me has been—friendly."

"Oh, for God's sake, Catherine, that is not what this is all about. I was hoping, dammit, that you might confide in me."

"Confide?" Her brows went up. "I have nothing to confide, sir."

"Stop it, blast you. I happen to know that you are no relation of the Pickerings. And what is more, even though nothing my aunt does can be considered odd, since eccentricity is her natural métier, it does seem wonderful that she would, for no apparent reason, suddenly remove all of you to Bath. And then there is this business of your hair."

"What about my hair?" she bristled.

"Oh, not that it does not look most becoming. Did I not say as much? But I can't help but wonder if your motivation was to change your appearance."

"Of course it was. Did I not say as much?"

"Don't fence with me, Catherine. I am talking about disguise, and you dashed well know it."

"Disguise? What an odd idea. I can assure you that I have no desire to disguise myself."

He grasped her shoulder, pulled her closer, and looked intently into her eyes. She quickly looked away. "I was hoping you could confide in me," he said huskily. "I know that we have only recently met. But you must also realize that I have, ah, er, certain feelings for you. I want to help you, Catherine. Can you not trust me?"

For a moment she appeared to waver. Then she resolutely pulled herself away. "La! Really, your lordship." She did not quite achieve the light tone she strove for. "If I had known your imagination would run amok merely because of a simple impulse on my part, I should never have dyed my hair. Now, if you will excuse me, I have an appointment with Miss Addie."

With acute disappointment reflected in his face, he watched her walk away. At the doorway she turned. "There is one more thing I should say."

"Yes?"

"About the—certain feelings—for me which you mentioned."

"Yes?"

"You must rid yourself of them. You see, they will not do."

She left the room quickly then, before he could answer.

Chapter Fourteen

"YOU STILL HERE, JEREMY?" LADY LAVINIA, A MIN-ute or so later, found him rooted to the spot. "Yes. We need to talk. Seriously."

"If you intend to lecture me about the hobby horse, don't bother. I never wish to see one of those machines again. That little extortionist was delighted I had broken it. I certainly know crocodile tears when I see them. He held me up for twice its original price. So if you are thinking of ringing a peal over me, forget it."

"Oh, damn all hobby horses!"

"My sentiments exactly. Now, if you will excuse me."

"I will do no such thing." He quickly strode around her to close the library door. "And you know it's not hobby horses I wish to discuss, aunt. We need to talk about Catherine."

"Catherine? Catherine?" Her eyebrows rose. "Are you not making very free with the Christian name of a young lady whom you have just met?"

"Oh? And how else should I address my cousin? Checkmate, I think, your ladyship."

She looked momentarily disconcerted, then quickly rallied. "The relationship is quite distant."

"The relationship is nonexistent. Come, sit down. I won't keep you long, but I think you had best tell me what you are up to."

She followed, reluctantly, to a sofa near the empty fireplace and sat beside him. "This is a waste of both our time. I am not 'up to' anything."

"Who is Catherine?" The blue eyes impaled her.

She sighed and capitulated. "I really cannot answer your question, Jeremy. All I can say is, I went to the registry to engage an upstairs maid and found her among the applicants. Despite the atrocious accent she had assumed, it was obvious that she was not servant class. Everything about her— her clothes, her bearing, her hands—bespoke quality. Certainly no one else would hire anyone so patently unsuited to domestic service, so I did."

"Yes, you would." He shook his head with mock despair, but his eyes were admiring.

"And since it seemed absurd to continue that particular charade here in Bath, I thought it best to present her as a relation.

"I had hoped, you see, that when we became better acquainted, she would confide in me. But she has not chosen to do so. So, since it is obvious that she is running away from something, and since I had had the notion for some time of starting a club for genteel ladies keen for new experiences, I thought it best to leave London. And Bath seemed fairly out of the way.

"So now you know as much about the young lady as I do. Need I ask you to keep what I have said confidential? We must respect Catherine's privacy. I am quite convinced that she will tell us her story in due time. But in the meantime, Jeremy, keep your distance. Oh, no need to look offended. I have seen your moon-calf expression when you look at her. But she is off limits. It is easy to see why you would become infatuated. She is a lovely young woman in every sense of the word. But until we know her history, you must not allow yourself to become romantically involved."

Easy enough to say. But he left those words unuttered. Instead, "I think I do know her history," he told her. "That is why I came haring down from London. To warn you. Do you happen to know a Lord Monkhouse?"

"Clarence Tilney, you mean?" She sniffed with distaste.

"No. That was the father, I think. The present Lord Monkhouse is *Hugh* Tilney. Monk, they call him. And a thoroughly bad lot he is, if there ever was one."

"I am not surprised. The Tilneys were all a bad lot. But what has this to do with Catherine?"

"I'm getting to that. You remember Chuffy Crews?" She nodded. "Well, a friend of Chuffy's attended Monk's wedding at St. Clement's a few weeks back. The church was packed, he said. People may not like the Tilneys, but they are one of the old families, you realize. Nobody seemed to know much about the bride, though. Her name was Fairclough, by the bye. Chuffy's friend couldn't recall the Christian name, if he ever knew it. Nor could he describe her. She wore a lace veil, you see. Anyhow, the ceremony went off as scheduled. Then immediately afterward the bride made some excuse to return to the vestry. When she did not come out after a reasonable period of time, they investigated, and she was gone. All they discovered was an open window and a wedding veil tossed behind the hedges. The story they put about was that she had been abducted. There is a fortune there, it seems. But Chuffy's friend is of the opinion that she scampered."

There was a long silence. Lavinia sat frowning at the floor. He waited patiently for her to speak.

"You say the church was crowded?"

"Chuffy said so."

"Then there is a lot of talk."

"It's the *on-dit* of the moment. But not in Monk's hearing. His temper is notorious. And he has the hue and cry out, Aunt Lavinia. He is determined to find her. He won't leave a stone unturned. Including those in Bath."

"I see." She was remembering her conversation with Colonel Marston while they had waited impatiently for Addie to appear. "That old bore of a colonel kept going on and on about how Catherine reminded him of someone. You do not suppose?"

"God knows. But the point is, if she is the bride—and you must admit that it appears likely—"

"I fear so."

"Then it is only a matter of time until *someone* puts two and two together. I think, Aunt Lavinia, that it is time we all went abroad."

"Nonsense."

"Not in the least. It seems dashed sensible to me."

"Then you cannot have thought. Monkhouse is bound to have the ports watched. And furthermore, *we* have nothing to say in the matter, for you will not become involved."

"The devil I won't!"

"You will not!" She glared. "For if Catherine is this young lady, her position will be made only more difficult by a love-smitten swain dangling after her. There must be no further hint of scandal. It will make her situation much more straightforward if she ran away merely because of an aversion to the marriage. I do not wish it to appear that you are in any way involved. Of course," she mused, "we should not dismiss the possibility that there is some other man that she is in love with."

He paled a bit. "I have, of course, thought of that. It does not alter the fact that I wish to help her."

She nodded. "Your sentiments do you credit. Still, until Catherine herself sees fit to confide in me, I feel that my hands are tied. I will, however, see to it that we drop out of sight for a while."

"Good. What do you have in mind?"

"Nothing as yet. But I will think of something." She rose to her feet, dismissively.

"Yes, you always do. You will let me know when you have decided, will you not?"

"I very much doubt it," she said reflectively. And then more firmly, "No, Jeremy, I will not. I do not think it for the best."

She turned a deaf ear on his protests and escorted him to the door.

Chapter
Fifteen

COLONEL MARSTON WAS A MAN POSSESSED OF proper family feelings. Still, it was not easy to suppress a groan as he watched his sister's eldest son threading his way among the leather chairs of the Senior United Service Club library. The truth was, the colonel did not care for his nephew above half. And, the business that had brought him to the metropolis completed, he had hoped for a glass of port with a few old cronies while they swapped war stories. A conversation with his sister's pride and joy could end only one way, with a request for funds on his nephew's part.

In spite of these impediments to sociability, when the young man had flopped uninvited in the chair beside his uncle's, Marston's "How are you, me boy?" sounded genuinely sympathetic. For in truth, the colonel was shocked at the young man's appearance. He mentally ticked off gaunt, haggard, drawn. But then *dissipated* sneaked into the inventory as the colonel took note of the bloodshot eyes and the premature lines beginning to mar the handsome countenance. It was clear Monk had been shooting the cat on a regular basis, Marston thought. Still, it was, he collected, only natural under the circumstances.

Lord Monkhouse waited until a waiter had materialized with another wineglass and filled it from the decanter on the small table by his uncle's elbow before he answered. "How the devil would a man be whose bride made a complete fool of him?" he growled.

The colonel glanced around to see if anyone could overhear. The dozen or so occupants of the room were, however, widely scattered. "No need to take that attitude. The poor girl could hardly help herself. And she certainly did not make a fool of you. Expect you have heard from the abductors by now. So," he added delicately, "if there is any difficulty about raising the blunt for ransom, you can always count on me, m'lad."

"Don't talk like a sapskull, uncle." Monkhouse tossed off the contents of his glass and poured another.

"I should point out that I do not care for your tone, sir." The colonel was at his most military.

"Sorry." Monkhouse passed his fingers through his hair to the detriment of its careful arrangement. "Shouldn't have snapped at you that way. Thought you knew, that's all. She wasn't abducted."

"She wasn't?" The colonel's chin dropped in astonishment. "Then what?"

"She bolted."

"My God! But why?"

"Who knows. Women!" Monkhouse's lip curled. "It would take a Solomon to figure out how their minds work. She had told her aunt and uncle she didn't wish to get married. Said we needed more time. We were rushing into things."

"Well, were you?"

"Lord, no. We were betrothed as children."

"Yes, but how well did you know each other?"

"Can't see what that has to say to anything. We had the rest of our lives, didn't we?"

"Well," the colonel mused, "I don't pretend to understand the fairer sex, but I expect that she panicked. Marrying a stranger and all. Given time, she should come around."

"You think so, do you?" the nephew sneered. "Well, she's had time. Four weeks without a word. And I for one don't believe the little baggage panicked. I think she ran to some lover somewhere. And when I find her, I'll kill him."

Marston looked alarmed. "Oh, I say now. No need to go off half-cocked. Seems to me that under the circumstances, the thing to do is to let her go. It ain't as though the marriage will be binding, without you actually—well, you know what I mean. If you are sure she ain't in need of rescue, well, my advice is to forget all about her and have the thing annulled. Then get on with your life."

"And lose a fortune? Damned if I will. Besides"— the handsome face turned ugly—"I will not be made a fool of."

"Actually, don't see what you can do about it, m'boy. If you haven't found her in all this time, well—"

"Oh, I'll find her. If it takes the rest of my life, I'll find her. And that's why I wished to talk to you, Uncle. I am asking some people who can keep their own counsel and not give the gossip-mongers more to chew on to help me find her. Understand you're spending some time in Bath. Could you keep a sharp eye out?"

"Well, yes, I suppose so." The colonel looked uncomfortable with this assignment. "But the truth is, I doubt I would recognize the girl if I bumped into her. Saw her only at the wedding, don't you know. And what with the veil and all. Well, all brides look deuced alike, now, don't they?

"Still, though," he reflected, "oddly enough, I did see someone who reminded me of someone I couldn't place, and now I realize that it was your bride I was thinking of."

Monkhouse spilled the port that he was pouring. He set the decanter down with a shaking hand. "You saw her?" he croaked hoarsely. "Where?"

"No, no. Of course not. What I said was I was *reminded* of her. Though I didn't know it was her I was reminded of. But it does go to show that I must have seen your bride a bit better than I thought. So possibly I could recognize her."

Monkhouse reached over to grab his uncle's shoulder and give it a shake. "Where was the girl?" His raised voice caused newspapers to be lowered and curious heads to turn.

"Here now. Get hold of yourself." His uncle detached the frenzied grip and frowned disapprovingly. "I said there was a resemblance, that's all. If that. This was not Miss—whatever your bride's name was."

"Fairclough." Monkhouse made a supreme effort to speak civilly. "Just tell me who it was that reminded you of her. And why."

"Actually, it was a young kinswoman of Lady Pickering's. So you can see that there is no reason for you to get into such a pucker. Couldn't be the same girl at all. And as for why, dashed if I know. For now I think on it, didn't your lady have yellow hair?"

"Something like."

"Well then, you see. This one has brown hair. Nothing like your bride at all, most likely. And, as I said, she is a Pickering."

"Lord Jeremy Pickering's family, is it?"

"Why, yes. Lady Lavinia's his aunt, in fact. And," he mused, "wouldn't surprise me if there wasn't something brewing there. Between Lord Jeremy and the young lady, I mean. He appeared to be rather smitten. At least that is the impression I got. Can't say I blame him. She's a fetching little thing. And has no connection with your missing bride. Take me word for it."

The colonel, with difficulty, then managed to change the subject. He was holding forth on the efficacy of the Bath waters when he interrupted himself. "Oh, I say." He was squinting toward the doorway, where an elderly man stood looking about the room. "Is that Bucky Farnsworth? Haven't seen him since we were on the Peninsula together." Marston half rose in his chair to wave at his friend. "You will excuse me, Monk m'boy. Would like to have a comfortable cose with Bucky. Old campaigners, don't you know. Would bore you to distraction. But I will promise to keep an eye out and all that. But my advice still is, forget it. Put the whole thing behind you. Nice chatting with you, m'boy."

Monkhouse delayed only long enough to pocket the bank notes which his uncle had surreptitiously slipped into his hand.

* * *

Upon his return to Bath, Colonel Marston's first act was to join the Pump Room throng, supposedly to drink his usual course of the waters. But his eyes lighted and his heart beat faster when he spied Mrs. Oliver with her two friends promenading the circumference of the room.

After he had persuaded them to join him at a table (an invitation that Mrs. Oliver accepted eagerly, Mrs. Abingdon with Christian resignation, and Lady Lavinia with little grace) and had inquired after Miss Pickering, who was visiting the lending library and would join them later, he confided that he had been more than glad to see the last of London. "The town's bare of company," he explained. "And it's my opinion that the place is dashed unhealthy at this time of year. Said as much to me nephew when I saw him. The poor fellow's been under quite a strain of late. Personal problems. Looks the very devil, if you'll pardon an old soldier's plain speaking. So I suggested he come to Bath and try the waters. Never thought, actually, that he would take me up on it." To the listening ladies he sounded a bit regretful. "You know how young people are. Brighton more likely to be his sort of thing. But damned—dashed, that is—if he didn't follow my advice. Will be joining me in a day or two."

"Oh, how nice for you," Addie cooed. "I wonder if we know him. Of course, if his name is also Marston, I do not. At least I do not recall ever having met anyone by that name before you."

"Oh, no, no. It's me sister's child. Tilney's the family name. But actually me nevvy is Lord Monkhouse."

There was a sudden crash, a splash, and a shattering of glass as Lady Lavinia dropped her water goblet.

Chapter
Sixteen

ALTHOUGH SHE DID NOT TERM IT SO, LADY LAVINIA called an emergency meeting of the Pickering Club for five o'clock that afternoon. In the meantime, she busied herself in a round of activities that made her usual neck-or-nothing pace seem leisurely. The clock was in the act of striking five when in lieu of gavel she pounded an ink pot (fortunately empty) upon the table. It had been a near thing. She had rushed into the house only seconds before. But the strands of jet hair that had slipped their moorings to escape the entrapments of her cap and a slight breathlessness were the only testaments to her whirlwind rounds. Her face was calmly resolute as she faced the threesome staring at her warily.

"Ladies"—she had risen from her chair to address them formally—"whereas our interlude here in Bath has been pleasant, and, in keeping with the high ideals of the Pickering Club, not entirely without educational value, I feel that we are now in danger of succumbing to the same ease of living and monotony of routine that made it necessary to leave the cocoon of London. That is why I think it imperative that we once more burst our bonds and try out our wings."

She paused dramatically. Those two members of the rank and file who knew her best were now gazing at her ladyship with alarm.

"I firmly believe that we shall never achieve our purpose of exploring the varied aspects of life while we simply change location without changing our mode of living. The Pickering Club should demand more of itself than that. So this is what I now propose."

After she had outlined her plan, there was a period of stunned silence. Addie broke it. "But I like it here in Bath!" she wailed. "I would not wish to leave under any circumstances. And what you are proposing is—is—utterly—" Words failed her.

Jane had put down the tambouring with which she had fortified herself and was gazing intently at her old friend's face. Some clue she spied in it stopped her protests cold. She sighed and capitulated. "You might as well save your breath to cool your porridge, Addie. It's plain that Lavinia has quite made up her mind. Besides, I don't suppose that this scheme will last forever. Or will it, Lavinia?"

"No, no. Of course not. We will merely remain away long enough to give our experiment ample scope and then we shall return here. After all, I have hired this house for the summer."

If two of the Pickerings had only managed a martyred resignation to their leader's scheme, the youngest member more than compensated for their lack of enthusiasm. Catherine was looking at Lady Lavinia with shining eyes. Respect was rapidly rising to near adulation. "I think her ladyship's proposal is famous," she declared. "I for one can hardly wait to try the Gypsy life."

The leader felt it necessary to speak a few cautionary words about their preparations. "Remember, we are embarking upon the simple life. We are not to encumber ourselves with the unnecessary trappings of a decadent civilization. I myself have made most of our preparations this afternoon. Now, here are the lists of personal things that you may take along." She handed out three slips of paper. "Pray confine your packing to these items."

When their eyes focused upon item number one, the club uniform, there were two failed attempts at insurrection. "This is the outside of enough," Addie wailed.

"I am not the trousers type, Lavinia," Jane seconded.

"Believe me," their leader replied frostily, "you will thank me later for this decision. Oh, and one other thing," she added as she picked up the ink pot, preparing to adjourn the meeting. "I must insist that you speak to no one of our plans. The servants will tell visitors that we have been called away suddenly on family matters. Now then"—she nipped in the bud the protest that was forming upon Addie's lips—"I declare the meeting of the Pickering Club adjourned."

The trio filed obediently out of the library to begin the preparations stipulated on their lists. Only

Jane was rebel enough, or else motivated sufficiently by an innate sense of self-preservation, to pen a hurried note to Lord Jeremy and then bribe a footman to deliver it after they had gone.

Since fashionable Bath was not given to early rising, the ton were spared the sight of four erstwhile respectable ladies (three of whom were clearly old enough to know better) dressed as pageboys, trudging through the town, lumbered with portmanteaus. The quartet was of considerable interest, however, to crossing sweeps, milk vendors, cats' meat men, and others of their ilk who stopped their employment to gape, to snicker, or to make rude remarks according to each one's natural inclination.

Lady Livinia's troops had gotten no farther than Pulteney Bridge which crossed the Avon River on the edge of town before two of them grew mutinous. "My feet hurt, Lavinia," Addie wailed pitifully, only to receive a curt "Serves you right for always buying your shoes too small" in reply.

"I collect you will be equally as sympathetic if I observe that my arms are about to fall off," Jane commented waspishly as she shifted her bulging bag from her right hand to her left.

"I told you to travel light," the leader retorted.

"Oh, do let me take that for you." Catherine grasped Jane's portmanteau by the handle. "I do not mind carrying it in the least."

"No, dear. Thank you very much, but I am quite determined to drop in harness, as it were."

"Oh, do stop your whining, please. It is not much farther now to our transportation."

"Transportation? We have transportation?"

Addie's face brightened like the rising sun. The sun eclipsed, however, as they came into sight of Bathwick Hill. "Oh, my goodness," Addie breathed.

"Oh, surely not!" Jane expostulated. "Not even you, Lavinia, would bring us to that."

That was a small, narrow-wheeled wagon, once, no doubt, of a bright, gay red but now a scabrous mess of peeling paint. Its bed was surmounted by a filthy, tattered canvas stretched tentlike over three arched staves. Between the shafts attached to this contraption stood an ungainly creature that could be loosely classified as a horse. Ribs were its most prominent feature. Its head was down while it cropped feebly at any grass within its range.

A swarthy Romany-type, as dirty and disreputable as the wagon, stood by the animal with a hand upon its bridle. He stared unblinkingly at the approaching ladies. His expression gave away none of his thoughts.

The same could not be said for Lady Lavinia. Indignation was written large upon her countenance as she surveyed the equipage she had purchased. "You promised me a strong horse and a stout wagon," she barked accusingly.

"And that's what I delivered." The Gypsy was unruffled by her tone. "This beast may not be handsome, but he's all heart, he is."

"He would have to be, would he not," her ladyship snapped back, "since there's not an ounce of flesh upon him."

"Too much fat don't make for good traveling." The Gypsy's eyes flicked Jane's way as he offered this opinion.

She bridled and dropped her portmanteau with a thud. "Well, at least I understand why you didn't have this equipage call for us at the Crescent, Lavinia." She sat down on the ground next to her bag.

"Oh, you poor, pitiful creature." Catherine had gone to the horse's head and was cooing sympathetically as she stroked its muzzle. The animal raised its head to gaze at her with dull brown eyes. She glared the Gypsy's way. "There are whip scars on this animal. There should be laws against mistreating beasts in this fashion."

His reply was to turn and hold out his hand toward Lady Lavinia as she emerged through the flap of canvas that served as a doorway to the interior of the wagon. "I'll take the rest of the blunt we agreed on. Half then, half on delivery, you said."

"I agreed to pay for a healthy animal and a wagon loaded with supplies."

"There's supplies in there," he said sullenly.

"You play fast and loose with the term, sir. But as you no doubt counted upon, beggars cannot be choosers. Here you are, then." She dropped some coins into his palm. He squinted at them and growled in protest. "You're a crown short."

"And you are making an exorbitant profit at that, as you are well aware of. The footpads could take lessons in thievery from you, sir. And the only reason I am allowing you to get away with highway robbery is to rescue that poor beast from your custody. Now, be gone before I change my mind and report you to the authorities."

He left, muttering in a strange, unintelligible language. Lady Lavinia did not need a translator, however, to know that he was calling down curses upon her head.

Chapter
Seventeen

"COME," LAVINIA SAID GRIMLY. "WE HAVE NO TIME to spare if we hope to make camp before nightfall. I owe you all a sincere apology. It is not my custom," she informed Catherine, "to buy a pig in a poke this way. But since time was of the essence and it is not in my nature either to look with suspicion upon a fellow human being (she ignored the derisive snort that came from Jane's direction), I decided to trust that brigand to make arrangements for us. I have learned my lesson. But it grieves me that my friends must suffer the consequences of—Jane! Whatever do you think you are doing?"

Jane had climbed into the wagon bed and was seated with her legs dangling out the back.

"What does it look like I'm doing? You did say that we've no time to spare."

"You surely cannot expect that poor beast to pull your weight."

"Oh, no, of course not. I am expecting to carry *him*. Forgive my naiveté, Lavinia, but I did think that the general idea of purchasing a wagon was for transportation. And I'll thank you to refrain from rude remarks concerning my weight."

"Oh, for heaven's sake, stop being so sensitive. I was not casting any aspersions. It should be obvious that this poor, half-starved creature cannot pull any of us. In fact, he cannot manage the load now hitched to him."

As Jane slid mutinously off the wagon bed, Lavinia crawled inside it. Her head shortly reappeared beneath the canvas flap. "We cannot spare much, but the firewood is expendable. We can always gather more in the forest. Come help me unload this, Jane."

"Oh, do let me do that," Catherine offered.

"No, no. You are holding the horse."

"Expect it to bolt, then, do you?" Jane asked testily.

"No need to be sarcastic. Catherine is getting the animal's trust. This is most important after the abuse the poor creature has suffered."

"And speaking of abuse—" Jane hurled a length of tree branch into the roadside ditch.

The two ladies soon had the wagon lightened and the horse, with Catherine's spoken encouragement and with Addie walking ahead while dangling a wilted carrot before its nose, was coaxed haltingly up the hill.

The Gypsy had assured Lady Lavinia that a wagon road led into Bathwick Wood. This did not prove an out-and-out prevarication. Traces of such a road did indeed exist, thick with undergrowth and replete with ruts. It soon became necessary to abandon the wagon altogether. "We will carry what we can with us," the president of the Pickering Club announced grimly, "and return for the rest after we have found a campsite."

Lavinia herself took charge of the large, blackened three-legged pot the Gypsy had provided. She quickly filled it with the turnips and wilted carrots that she found in a gunnysack. One sniff of a dressed hare the Gypsy had supplied caused her to abandon any notion of rabbit stew. "Keep a sharp eye out for edible greens, herbs, nuts, berries, and the like as we go along," she told her troops. "If soldiers can live off the land, so can Pickerings." Her bravado dimmed a bit, however, as she hoisted the cast-iron pot and her elderly knees buckled.

The ladies made a weird procession as they threaded and beat their way deeper into the wood. Each carried as many of the Gypsy's supplies as they could manage. Plus her portmanteau, Jane half carried, half dragged the wagon's canvas covering which Lavinia insisted they remove. Addie limped along, draped in blankets, carrying her own and Catherine's bags. Catherine was leading the horse with one hand while, over Lavinia's protest, sharing the weight of the iron pot. Their progress was impeded more than once by the necessity of putting this vessel down while Lavinia pounced upon some questionable provender of nature.

"You do know she is going to poison us all, do you not?" Addie remarked conversationally as she sat down upon a cushion of moss to remove her half-boots and massage her toes while she watched Lavinia add a dozen wild mushrooms to the pot.

"I wouldn't worry," Catherine said kindly. "I am convinced that Lady Lavinia knows exactly what she is doing."

Jane gave the young woman a jaundiced look. *She is actually enjoying this* was her conclusion.

It was true. The deeper into the woods they went, the more Catherine seemed to come alive. Her eyes sparkled. And the look she bent upon her ladyship was almost worshipful.

The ladies resumed their march and trudged in silence for a bit while Jane recalled old fairy tales concerning helpless babes who became lost in woods not nearly as thick and wild, she wagered, as this very one. She was just considering gathering pebbles to mark their trail when the horse astonished them all by whinnying.

"My word! I did not suspect he had enough ginger in him to actually give tongue!" Addie exclaimed.

"He smells water," Lavinia replied. "As my nephew would say, I will bet a monkey on it. Ah, yes. There it is." They had broken out into a grassy clearing, dissected by a lively, gurgling brook. "Ah, at last! At least that larcenous Gypsy got one thing right."

The pastoral scene was idyllic enough to enthrall even the most resistant for a moment. For a moment was all their leader allotted to the sparkling water and fern-filled banks, to the grassy expanse on either side, strewn with wildflowers, bordered by trees. She began to bark out orders with an authority that the Iron Duke of Wellington might have envied.

"Food and shelter are the first orders of the day. Jane, you are to gather dry firewood. But keep an

120

eye out for nature's edibles as you do so. Addie, since your feet are no doubt blistered by now, you may soak them in the stream while at the same time scrubbing those miserable excuses for vegetables the thieving Gypsy left us. Catherine—ah, yes, well done." The leader nodded her approval as she watched the young woman tether the horse amid ample grazing. "You and I will go back to the wagon and fetch whatever supplies we can carry. But first . . ." She opened her portmanteau and produced a long length of string with a hook attached. Then, after upending several stones at the water's edge, she exposed some singularly repulsive-looking grubs, the juiciest of which she attached to the hook, though not without an expression of disgust, several attempts, and a pricked finger. She then proceeded to tie the string onto a willow branch that was trailing in the water. "There now." She rose from her muddy knees with satisfaction. "Supper should be on the hook by the time we return."

"You certainly must anticipate cooperative fish," Jane scoffed as she set about her own assignment. "If that is all there is to it, Izaak Walton certainly wasted his time writing a whole book on the subject." Disregarding Lavinia's speaking look, she reentered the wood and began picking up fallen limbs while making sure that her wanderings did not carry her beyond the sound of the murmuring brook. Once assured that she was out of sight of her fellow campers, she dumped her armload of sticks upon the ground and sat down herself to lean back against the smooth tree trunk and extract a chocolate from the hoard she had concealed about her person. She sighed and munched contentedly for a bit. "I could teach our intrepid leader a thing or two about survival," she informed the curious gray squirrel who eyed her from a tree branch above her head.

By the time the moon rose over Bathwick Wood, the spirits of even the more reluctant campers had risen as well. The canvas had been stretched on ropes between two trees, a mulberry bush, and a rather wobbly tent stake improvised from one of the longer sticks Jane had gathered for firewood. They would be sheltered from any rain that fell. The bed coverings the Gypsy had provided had proven to be clean, a state of affairs Lady Lavinia had not really hoped for. A fire, thanks to the large quantity and the dryness of the wood Jane had gathered (she had tried unsuccessfully to look modest under Lavinia's fulsome praise), crackled merrily underneath the iron pot which, after several disheartening collapses, was suspended by a length of chain supported by a tripod of stout branches. There had even been a fish wiggling upon Lavinia's hook. *Minnow* would have described it best, Jane observed caustically, though privately she was more than a little impressed. "Size is not everything," Lavinia had replied as she scaled and gutted the slippery fish with a hunting knife she first whetted upon a stone to a very satisfactory sharpness. "It will add flavor and nutrients to the stew."

Now, as the foursome sat around the fire, listening to the bubbling of the pot, the chattering of the brook, the symphony of the creatures of the night, and the back and forth communications of a distant pair of owls, a feeling of well-being stole over the little group. Catherine voiced it. "Oh, this is famous. It really is. What a wonderful adventure you have planned, Lady Lavinia."

"Here! Here!" Addie and Jane exclaimed to their mutual surprise.

The four ladies sat in silent contentment a little longer. Then Addie began to sniff the breeze inquisitively. Catherine joined in. "What is that peculiar odor?" she asked.

After a few exploratory sniffs, Lavinia offered her opinion. "I expect that there is a stagnant pond somewhere in the vicinity."

"I think not." Jane, in the true Pickering Club spirit of scientific research, rose to put her hypothesis to the test. She walked over to the bubbling kettle, then stooped to sniff. She quickly backed away to clap her handkerchief over her nostrils and make a muffled observation.

"That, ladies, is our supper that you smell."

Chapter
Eighteen

"WHAT DO YOU MEAN, THEY'VE GONE?" LORD Jeremy raised his voice and glared at his aunt's temporary butler. "Where to and for how long?"

The butler did not have the privilege of glaring back. His recourse was to reach new heights of starchiness. "As to that, I could not say, sir. Her ladyship did not choose to make me privy to her plans."

"The devil she didn't!" Lord Jeremy now realized that if it was information he wished, he would be wiser to take a new tack altogether. He got himself in hand. "Just tell me anything you know, Wilcox," he said pleasantly.

They were standing in the hall of Number 3, the Royal Crescent. Lord Jeremy had spent a restless night. As a result of so much tossing and turning, he had overslept and gone rushing from his hotel. He had looked first in the Pump Room, then walked on to the Crescent, hoping for a moment alone with his newfound "cousin."

For Lord Jeremy, at three A.M. or thereabouts, had decided upon the direct approach. He would ask Catherine point-blank if she was Monkhouse's missing bride. And being so resolved, it had taken the wind out of his sails to find that the birds had flown.

"I have told you everything I know, sir." The butler traded in some of his starchiness for injured sensibility. "Her ladyship merely said that the four of them were leaving for an indefinite period. And when I asked what I should answer to inquiries concerning their whereabouts, I was told to say that they had been called away suddenly on business. There was no need, she informed me, to be any more forthcoming.

"But as for that—" the butler began, then snapped his teeth together against possible indiscretion.

"Yes?" Jeremy said encouragingly.

"Why, nothing, m'lord. I just found it rather odd, that's all."

Jeremy looked at the older man shrewdly. "I say, Wilcox, if you are afraid that even a syllable of our conversation will reach my aunt's ears, you may rest easy. My lips are sealed. Now, tell me. What was odd?"

"Why, the way they were dressed, sir. I must say that none of the ladies in any of the households where I have been employed would have dreamed of appearing in public looking like that. And I can assure you, sir, that I have been in the employ of some of our best families."

"Yes, I am sure you have." Jeremy spoke soothingly. "Their manner of dress was odd, you say? Don't tell me. Pageboy costumes?"

"Something of the kind, I collect," the butler sniffed. "I don't mind saying I was relieved when they left the house before any of the quality were likely to be stirring. But I do not care to think what those in service might be saying if they chanced to see them."

While pretending to sneeze, Jeremy managed to hide a grin with his handkerchief. "Regular spectacle, were they?" he asked when he'd recovered. "Well, never mind. It will certainly not reflect upon you, Wilcox. After all, you are only temporarily in my aunt's employ.

"Now, are you quite sure that her ladyship did not leave some message for me? With her maid perhaps?"

"Quite sure, sir. I asked most particularly."

And with that Jeremy had to be content. His head was down and he was thinking furiously as he left. As a result, he almost collided with two gentlemen coming up the steps.

"Well, well. As I live and breathe, Lord Jeremy Pickering. Now, it certainly is a small world, as folk are fond of saying."

Jeremy's head jerked up, and he looked straight into the suspicious eyes of Lord Monkhouse.

Lord Jeremy's emotions ran a speedy gamut through dismay, fear, and all the way to rage. It was a struggle, but when he replied, he somehow managed to sound nonchalant.

"My word, it's Monkhouse. Last person in the

world I would expect to see in Bath. What brings you to this unfashionable watering hole, Hugh?"

"Familial affection. At least in part. I believe you know my uncle here."

The two gentlemen nodded to each other.

"Of course, I was also moved by curiosity."

"Oh, really? Well, there's little curious about Bath that I can see. No, I take that back. I do wonder how people can stomach those noxious waters."

Monkhouse's polite chuckle did not show in his eyes. "You have a point," he said. "But my curiosity has more to do with your—cousin."

"Really?" Jeremy managed to look amazed. "Catherine, you mean? Nothing odd about her that I know of. Well, at least there isn't if you take no notice of the squint. Which I don't, of course. Take notice, I mean."

"Squint? What squint?" Colonel Marston looked puzzled. "I never noticed any squint."

"Oh, did you not? Well, *squint* is not exactly the mot juste, now that I think of it. The fact is, one eye is prone to wander a bit. Actually," he hurried on to say, "it ain't all that unattractive. Just makes it a bit difficult at times to tell who she's addressing."

"That's strange." Monkhouse's own eyes narrowed. "The colonel here assures me she is a nonpareil."

"Oh, really?" Jeremy looked astonished. "Oh, I say, sir, you *have* been in Bath too long. Still, I probably don't do Catherine justice. You know how it is with cousins. We were in leading strings together. And she was a perfect terror of a child. Perhaps as a consequence I am still prone to view her as a quiz."

"That's also odd. My uncle here was of the opinion you two might make a match of it."

"Me and Catherine? My God! Oh, no, sir. A bad idea that, in my opinion. Cousins marrying, that is. Happens all the time, I know, but have you checked out some of the progeny? No, I would not wish to marry Catherine." He appeared to repress a shudder.

"Then let us hope that it will not happen," Monkhouse said dryly. "But why do I get the impression, Jeremy, that you protest too much? I am now more eager than ever to see this—cousin—of yours."

"Why on earth should you be?" Jeremy blurted out. "Didn't I hear that you were getting leg-shackled? I should think that—oh, my God!" He looked appalled. "Oh, I am sorry, old fellow. I have put my foot into it, haven't I? Never pay that much attention to gossip, you see. So I forgot all about the unfortunate— Do forgive me."

"Don't mention it." Monkhouse's smile was a mere baring of the teeth. "And don't let us detain you. Uncle, give a knock."

"Oh, no need for that," Jeremy said. "The ladies are not at home."

"Not at home?" The colonel looked perplexed. "But we were just in the Pump Room, looking for them. Where else could they be?"

"Out of town. At least that's what the butler told me."

"Out of town? Where?"

"You have me there, sir. Wilcox doesn't know."

"A likely story," Monkhouse growled.

"Possibly. But it seems to be the only one he has."

"Oh, really? Well, we shall see about that."
Monkhouse reached around his uncle to ply the
knocker. "Don't let us keep you."

"Well, no. Must toddle on." Jeremy brushed past
them down the steps, then turned. "Oh, I say,
Monk. If you are bored, and you must be since
you're here, they say there's a fetching little thing
who has a small part at the Theatre Royal. Girl by
the name of Sophy. You might want to— Oh, well,
perhaps not, then." Lord Monkhouse's expression
was not encouraging. "A bad idea, actually. Good-
bye now."

Lord Jeremy managed a leisurely stroll till he
was out of sight. He then took to his heels.

He arrived, breathless, back at the White Hart.
"Has there been a message for me?" he asked his
startled valet as he rushed into his room. Receiving
a negative reply, he collapsed in a wing chair by the
window, put his head in his hands, and tried to
think. Where the devil could they have gone? Back
to London? He did not think so. It was hard to tell
just how seriously Lavinia had taken his story of
Monk's absconded bride, but whether totally convinced or not that the bride and Catherine were
one and the same, his aunt would never put the
girl at even the slightest risk. Confound her ladyship, anyhow, he thought. It was one thing to be in-
dependent but quite another to carry the concept to
excess.

His fruitless reverie was interrupted by the valet
who reentered the room with a letter thrust forward on a salver. "This just came, sir. The footman
from the Crescent apologized for being so late de-
livering it. But he said the lady was most eager
that no one know she was writing you. So he had to

wait till he had an excuse to get away, in this case an errand for the cook."

The master snatched the message and the man tactfully withdrew. Jeremy broke the seal and felt a twinge of disappointment when he saw Jane's signature. Then he hastily devoured the contents. "Bathwick Wood," he exclaimed aloud. "Of all the hen-witted— Still—" He read the letter once again, taking special note of the conclusion:

Under no circumstance must Lavinia learn that I have written you. You know how she feels about females who think they must rely upon men for everything. But I will feel much more secure knowing that someone is aware of our whereabouts. Just do not betray me. A lifelong friendship could be at stake.

Chapter Nineteen

JEREMY'S FIRST REACTION WAS RELIEF THAT CATHERINE was safely out of harm's way. His next was fear that the nature party would return while Monkhouse was still in Bath. Well, surely that could be prevented. He would somehow locate the women and manage a private word with Jane. He would make her understand that under no circumstance must they return until he gave word that it was safe to do so.

Once resolved, he wasted no time, but called for his curricle to be sent around immediately. He should be able to locate four highly conspicuous women and be back in his hotel by dark.

Jeremy raced across Pulteney Bridge at a pace that sent the patrons of the shops that lined it leaping for safety. However, he did slow down when he reached Grove Street and spied a crowd collected before a building that looked just like any of the others in its row. It was actually the "new" prison, a name it had borne for fifty years or more.

It was impossible not to associate the crowds and curiosity with his aunt Lavinia, although common sense told him that the quartet was not likely to have been jailed. Their costumes might be a bit bizarre—well, actually a lot bizarre, but they were hardly indecent. Nonetheless, he slowed down his rig to inquire what was happening.

"Prisoner escaped, sir," one of the onlookers, a dustman, from his garb, answered him. "Liked to 'ave killed a guard, 'e did. The doctor's with the fellow now. Touch and go, they say."

"Good God!"

Jeremy looked horror-struck enough to assure the speaker of the dramatic impact of his recital. Still, he could not resist embellishment. "A real bad'un, this one is. Was to 'ave been sent to the hulks."

"Which way did he go, do you think?"

"Well now," the dustman's companion, a younger man clad in a dirty smock, chimed in with a grin, "if you 'ad just broke out of 'ere, which way would you go? Back to Milsom Street? Not bloody likely. 'E'll be 'eading in the same direction as you, most likely."

"Oh, dear God!"

The man in the smock grinned more broadly still as Jeremy sprang his cattle.

Finding Bathwick Wood was not a problem. Nor was it difficult to spot the wagon road. But the curricle made it only as far as the abandoned Gypsy wagon when Jeremy, too, concluded that from then on he would have to go on foot. He was not, however, quite as willing as the women to abandon his rig to the mercy of thieves—or escaped convicts. There was no comparison between his curricle, a recently purchased bang-up-to-the-nines affair, and their decrepit wagon. He therefore wasted considerable time backtracking to a farmhouse he had spotted shortly before entering the woods. The farmer there was more than willing to stable his horse and curricle for a handsome fee. He also supplied Jeremy with the news that, yes, he had seen four females—"freakish-looking" was the adjective he employed—along with a rackety Gypsy wagon. Reassured that he was in the right vicinity, no mistake, Jeremy hurried back the way that he had come.

After he had passed the wagon once again and penetrated deeper into the thickening forest, he had every reason to regret his impetuosity. Why had he gone tearing off like a maniac without provisions? Food topped his imaginary list as the day wore on and his stomach began to rumble. A compass also sprang to mind. Would he ever find his way out of this maze again? And a pistol would have been comforting. Every rustle of dry leaves brought to mind the horrid image of a desperate convict stalking him.

In vain Jeremy looked for indications that the women had passed the way that he was taking. But he had to admit that short of leaving signposts behind, there was no way they could have left a trail that he could read. Snapped twigs and crushed plants, the sort of things that were the very ticket in Indian lore, held no meaning in his case. His inclination was to shout "Aunt Lavinia, where the devil are you?" as loudly as he could. He was stopped from doing that, not so much from his scruples against betraying Jane as from the fear that any response might come from the escaped prisoner.

Darkness and desperation set in together. Jeremy, recognizing the futility of thrashing about in a pitch-black wood, settled down, uncomfortably propped against a tree. He managed to doze a bit, but soon awakened, stiff, confused, and cold. When he spied a faint flickering through the trees, he thought at first he was hallucinating. But when he rubbed his eyes and the glimmer did not fade, he followed it like a moth attracted to a flame.

His approach to the campsite would have been no less or no more stealthy if he could have known in advance whether he would find the ladies or the convict. But when he discovered that it was, indeed, the Pickering party, his relief was overwhelming.

He cowered behind a bush, trying to decide what to do. His mission had changed drastically since leaving the White Hart. Then, what he had intended was to have a private word with Jane before returning to Bath with all possible speed to keep an eye on Monkhouse till that scoundrel left the city. But now that a desperate convict was on the loose, his role had changed to that of male protector.

The problem was, he was ill-equipped for this assignment. He was ravenous, he was cold, and above all else, he was weaponless. He cursed himself once more for being so improvident.

By the flickering light of the fire he was able to ascertain that barring the advent of a desperate criminal, the women were in an enviable position. They were more or less sheltered from the elements with a canvas overhead and blankets wrapped around them. They appeared to be sleeping soundly. And they had food. He looked longingly at the iron pot suspended over the campfire. Surely it contained some sort of stew. He sniffed the air experimentally, but the breezes carried any aroma that there might be in the opposite direction. His imagination supplied the ingredients: some kind of meat—a fowl most likely—potatoes, leeks, parsnips. His mouth watered.

Well, he would be of no use in a crisis if he were weak with hunger. Or possibly even starved to death. How long would that take? They would not miss a cupful from the pot. Resolved, he stole stealthily into the ladies' camp.

First ascertaining that no one stirred beneath the canvas (he made note of the fact that his aunt was prone to snore), he tiptoed toward the pot and almost whooped aloud when he came near colliding with a pair of feet. His heart drummed in his ears from shock. He was amazed that the noise of it did not rouse the tenters, let alone Addie, whose feet he had almost stepped on. He silently cursed himself for not realizing that his aunt would have, of course, posted a guard. He was most fortunate that Addie had proved inadequate to the task. Her breathing now began to rival Lavinia's for volume. She was leaning back against the tree that had shielded her from his view with a blanket wrapped around her shoulders but not quite reaching her stockinged feet. Jeremy gently pulled the edge down to cover them. He then eased his way on toward the simmering black pot. He leaned well over it and drew in his breath. Then he quickly recoiled. And gagged. What was that noxious stuff? Filthy stockings? Insect repellent? Surely it did not come under the category of food. If the women had actually partaken of its contents, they might not be asleep, but poisoned. He looked anxiously at Addie. There was no mistaking her glow of health.

Jeremy gazed about him hungrily, then spied a

sack a little distance from the campfire. It contained only a few antique carrots. Still, beggars—or, in this case, robbers—could not be choosers. He stuffed them in the pocket of his Bond Street coat.

His eyes lighted up and he almost uttered a grateful "ah!" as he spotted the kitchen knife lying alongside the now-empty sack. It might be needed more for a weapon than as a cooking utensil. Feeling vaguely piratical, he tucked it into the waistband of his trousers.

Next he tiptoed toward the tent. His idea was, or so he told himself, to see if he could manage to awaken Jane. He soon saw that this would prove impossible. There was no hope of extracting one without rousing the other two. Thwarted in this objective, Jeremy stood for several seconds, staring down at Catherine's dimly perceived blanketed form. She lay on her side, facing him, her head resting upon her arm, her lips slightly parted, her breath soft and regular. Jeremy was unprepared for the rush of tenderness he felt at the sight of her lovely vulnerability. He stood spellbound for a bit, then forced himself to steal away. But just as he was turning to do so, he spied a packet lying next to Jane. He stooped to pick it up, then barely stifled an uttered *Eureka* when he found chocolates in his hand. He pocketed his treasure without a qualm, then stole back to his observation bush, where the sweetmeats sustained him throughout the remainder of the night.

Just before dawn Lord Jeremy thought it prudent to put more distance between the campsite and himself. He slipped silently away, following the course of the noisy little stream.

Chapter
Twenty

IT WAS JANE WHO FIRST DISCOVERED THAT ALL WAS NOT as it should have been. When she awakened, her hand groped sleepily by her side. Then she explored anxiously underneath her blanket. Next she sat up and looked at her rising tent mates accusingly. "Who took my chocolates?" she demanded.

"Chocolates!" Addie had awakened from sentry duty and was just entering the tent. "You have chocolates? And did not share? Well, of all the selfish, inconsiderate—"

"Never mind all that. The point is, who took them?"

"The point is, what kind of friend would bring along a hoard of chocolates and sneakily devour them while her comrades starve?"

"That will do," Lavinia intervened as the two bosom bows glared at each other. "No one is going to starve, Adelaide. As soon as you become really hungry and get over your finickiness, you will discover, as Catherine and I have, that my stew is most nutritious."

(Here Catherine barely restrained a shudder. She had been the only one who, out of loyalty, had partaken of the noxious-looking brew. The memory was not one she cared to recall so early in the morning.)

"Well, at least you have survived," Addie said crossly. "Which, I must say, relieves me. As for the chocolate hoarder, I daresay she did not suffer the hunger pangs that I have endured for the live-long night."

"Oh, I doubt you are all that starved. What is that famous line about Macbeth's wife? 'Methinks the lady doth protest too much?' I'll bet a monkey that you ate my chocolates while you were supposed to be keeping watch."

"I did not!"

"Children! Children! That will do," Lady Lavinia intervened with authority. "I am not sure, Jane, that I could find it in my heart to blame Adelaide if she has eaten your chocolates. For it does appear mean-spirited to bring along provisions and not share them. Not that I personally would have wished to abuse my body with sweetmeats when there was nutritious fare to be had. And I am certain that Catherine agrees. (Here Catherine could not quite meet her idol's eyes.) But what I think probably happened is that you ate the chocolates yourself sometime during the night and then forgot all about it."

"Fustian," Jane muttered.

"At any rate, the subject is closed. Let us go

make some tea and then we will all feel a great deal better. You had last watch, Addie. Is the fire still burning?"

"Of course." Addie, who had roused barely in time to revive it from mere embers, looked insulted.

After Lavinia had added more water from the brook to the contents of the iron pot (whose color and aroma had not improved from its all-night simmering), she decided to put the remaining vegetables in the mix. She peered into the empty sack and called to her fellow campers, who were washing their hands and faces in the stream. "Oh, I say. Did one of you happen to eat the leftover carrots?"

"*Et tu*, Lavinia?" Jane stood up, arms akimbo, and glared. "Who knows? Perhaps after I made an unconscious feast of chocolate I also sleepwalked and gobbled up those half-dead carrots."

"*I* certainly would not be so selfish," Addie sniffed.

"Why, no." Catherine alone seemed not to resent the question.

"Well, then," Lavinia observed heartily, "the chocolate mystery is solved. And I think you owe Addie an apology, Jane. For it is obvious that some marauding animal struck our camp last night and helped himself to whatever food was available."

An anxious discussion followed concerning the nature of the beast. Theories ranged all the way from fearsome bears to more compatible rabbits. But then Jane felt obliged to observe that while the latter hypothesis stood up quite well where carrots were concerned, she for one had not heard of a rabbit with a sweet tooth. This threw them back, reluctantly, upon bears.

Lady Lavinia had not joined in the discussion.

139

For she had failed to inform her party that a sharp knife was also missing. And the only animals she could think of who were attracted to that sort of thing were of the two-legged variety.

The sun was high in the sky before the ladies finished their breakfast. But the meal and the glorious morning had had a salubrious effect. The bickering had ceased.

"Oh, that was marvelous." Catherine licked her fingers inelegantly after she had devoured the last morsel. They had, to the amazement of Jane and Addie, found three fish wriggling upon the hooks and lines that Lavinia had set out the night before. And they had presented a united front to prevent her from throwing the trio into the cast-iron catchall. Instead, the fish had been cooked separately over the coals and ravenously devoured along with cups of scalding tea.

"Well, now," Lavinia declared when the meal concluded, "I suggest that the three of you go back to those bramble bushes we stumbled into in the dark last night." She looked down at the scratches on her arms, a painful reminder of the incident. "Gather what berries you can find there. I shall explore a bit in the meantime to see what other provender nature might provide."

"Shouldn't I come with you?" Catherine asked anxiously. "It might not be safe for you to wander about alone."

"Oh, no. No need of that. I will exercise caution, of course, but I am certain there is nothing to fear."

"I expect she is right," Addie muttered. "Any bears are certain to be by the berry bushes."

"I insist upon accompanying you." Catherine, it seemed, could be as strong-minded as Lady Lavinia. "None of us should wander about alone." She, too, had thought of the Gypsy.

The berry pickers left and Lavinia, with Catherine sticking to her like a leech, set off in the opposite direction. While pretending an interest in greens, nuts, and the like, she scouted the perimeters of the camp, keeping a weather eye out for the human animal who had stolen their knife. But they scared up nothing more sinister than a few squirrels and a chipmunk, none with chocolate on their breath. Satisfied that at least no one lurked in close proximity to their campsite, she enlarged her field of operation.

Lord Jeremy, about a mile downstream from the ladies, where a rude dam had trapped the waters into a pool, had not fared as well as they. His breakfast had consisted of half a carrot and the sole remaining chocolate. But even worse than hunger was indecision. After only one night alone in the woods, it had been borne in upon him that he was an urban, civilized man and no Robinson Crusoe. The notion of lurking near the women undetected, like some hovering guardian angel ready to spring to their aid in the event of a desperate convict attack, was beginning to lose a bit of its appeal. No, the best plan was to confront the campers, tell them all about the escaped convict, inform his aunt Lavinia privately about the Monkhouse threat, and guide them to a place of safety from both menaces.

Still, his conscience pricked him at the prospect of violating his "aunt" Jane's confidence. Lavinia would never forgive her for her betrayal. And Jane would never forgive him for his. He sighed and cracked one of the nuts he'd frightened a

141

squirrel into dropping, then picked out the meat while he pondered his problem. Just supposing that he had, by chance, learned of the convict's daring escape and had curiously joined the crowd gathered in front of the prison. Then suppose that someone in that crowd had mentioned seeing four outlandishly clad ladies pass by earlier and had voiced the hope that they did not meet up with the desperate escapee. Could he not have, after further inquiry, put two and two together? This, of course, had panicked him, and he had set out in hot pursuit, inquiring as he went whether anyone had seen either the convict or the ladies. A certain farmer had recalled four pageboys turning into Bathwick Wood. He had immediately plunged into the forest after them and now, after wandering all night and well into the morning, he had fortuitously stumbled upon their camp.

Not great, as stories went, perhaps, but possible. His shrewd aunt might suspect that he had been privy to their plans, but she could not be positive. That should let Jane off the hook. Besides, when Lavinia learned that Monkhouse was hot on Catherine's trail, she would have more important matters on her mind.

Having decided on a course of action, Jeremy turned his attention upon himself. He was, he realized, a sorry sight—filthy, with a ripped coat sleeve, the souvenir of an encounter with a broken tree limb, and with his boots mud-caked from an encounter with a bog. His cravat had lost its maharata arrangement hours before, and his general appearance smacked of having been dragged about by some enormous cat.

The once-fastidious Bond Street beau rubbed his hand over the stubble of his beard and groaned. The thought of Miss Catherine Pickering, or whatever her rightful name was, seeing him like this was dampening in the extreme.

Well, at least he could get the caked mud off his boots. He pulled them off and knelt down by the pool to wash them. Having completed this task satisfactorily (if one suppressed the need for blacking and a polishing cloth, that is), it occurred to him that a bath before coming into contact with the lady of his dreams would do no harm. The thought was quickly converted into action. Lord Jeremy stripped off his clothes, folded them neatly beneath a hawthorn bush, and dove into the frigid waters.

It was there that Lady Lavinia and Catherine Pickering discovered him.

Chapter
Twenty-one

WHEN THEY SPIED THE SWIMMER IN THE DISTANCE, he was no more than a ripple and a splash. Since she had taken it for granted that the prowler was the Gypsy, Lavinia's first reaction was "Well, he can certainly profit from a bathe." She wrinkled her nose distastefully at his memory. But as the swimmer moved still farther away, the two crept closer to the bank of the dammed-up stream. There they spied his discarded garments.

This was a mystery. They had expected to find the Gypsy's filthy rags. Here, instead, were the exquisitely tailored though sadly bedraggled coat, waistcoat, trousers, and linen of a veritable pink of the ton. Both ladies thrust their heads cautiously around the bush that concealed them to sneak another look at the cavorting bather. As the gentleman arced like a porpoise in the distance, a flash of white skin confirmed the fact that the bather was entirely nude. It took the emergence of the head and shoulders to confirm Lavinia's growing suspicion: The swimmer was indeed her nephew Jeremy.

Catherine had been at least as swift with an identification. Ladylike modesty told her not to stare. But ladylike modesty seemed entirely out of place in this environment. Her eyes widened.

On the other hand, Lavinia's black eyes narrowed. Her eyebrows met ominously. Righteous indignation engulfed her being. Obeying an impulse that she stopped to consider only later on, she gathered up Lord Jeremy's garments, carefully placing the knife concealed beneath them inside her own skirtband, and signaling Catherine to follow, melted, unseen, back into the woods.

"What do you plan to do with his clothes?" Catherine asked when they were well out of earshot.

"Keep them for a while" was the tight-lipped answer.

"But isn't that an odious trick to play?" Catherine giggled, though, in spite of herself.

"No more odious than to sneak into a camp of sleeping women and help oneself to their provisions."

"So *he* was the one."

"Oh, yes." Lady Lavinia picked up her pace. As the woods thickened, Catherine was forced to follow behind, Indian fashion.

"But surely a few chocolates and some carrots aren't worth—" Her activated conscience was subdued by the superior force of her ladyship's glare.

"It is not what he took that is at issue here. There is a principle involved. I cannot forgive the fact that he has been spying on us. Though perhaps," she qualified, "he is not entirely to blame. I can see my brother's fine Italian hand in all of this. For I cannot believe that Jeremy on his own would have left the metropolis for Bath. No, the more I think on it, the more I am convinced that the earl has put him up to this. He has never approved of my establishing my own household. For he is of the addle-pated opinion that no female can survive without some man, never mind how mutton-headed, to tell her what to do. Yes, I am positive that he has commissioned Jeremy to see what we are up to. Well, I shall prove to both of them that we women are far better prepared to survive on our own under primitive conditions than the so-called stronger sex."

When he emerged from his bathe, Jeremy's first thought was that the hardships of the wilds had softened his brain. It seemed that he was mistaken about which bush concealed his clothing. But after a frantic search beneath every shrub in the vicinity, he was forced to the logical conclusion: Someone had stolen it.

That much becoming clear, his reviving mind made another leap. The convict! Who else would be in dire need of a costume change?

Having forged ahead this far, his powers of reasoning then came up with a working hypothesis. The escaped convict had stolen the clothes to exchange for his prison garb. Ergo, he must have left his prison garb behind.

Jeremy spent several minutes beating those very bushes he had previously searched on the off chance that having been obsessed by his own purloined wardrobe, he might have overlooked any other garments left lying around. When nothing turned up at the water's edge, he expanded his search to the perimeters of the wood. Again, to no avail.

He finally sat down, carefully, upon a log and tried to decide what was best for him to do. Perhaps it was the fact that this familiar act proved so unfamiliarly uncomfortable that his thought processes gathered still more strength and then refocused. Up to this point his attention had been riveted upon one fact alone: He, Lord Jeremy Pickering, was buck naked here in Bathwick Wood.

But now he saw the real issue crystal-clearly. There was a desperate convict at liberty in the vicinity of the spot where his aunt, her two bosom bows, and the girl he feared he was in love with were camped. And he alone would have to save them from having their throats cut (he paled as he remembered the purloined knife) or from being subjected to a fate far worse. He leapt up from the log and began to run—gingerly, as his bare feet encountered all the customary debris of the forest— from pine cones to broken twigs—toward the ladies' camp.

When he neared the site he slowed down and moved in stealthily, motivated as much by modesty as from the fear of finding the convict already working his fiendish will. He covered the last few yards on hands and knees, then paused, trying not to breathe, to listen. All was silent. He parted the bushes to survey the scene.

It was serenity itself. The iron pot still stewed above the fire. Several pairs of stockings were drying upon a line hung near it. Four portmanteaus and four folded blankets were neatly arranged beneath the canvas awning. There was not a soul in sight.

Jeremy's blood ran even colder than the frigid state brought on by the disappearance of his clothing. His first thought was that the convict had captured the four women and removed them from the spot. Still, there was no sign of struggle, and it was difficult to believe that his aunt Lavinia would go peaceably. Perhaps they were merely out on a nature walk. If so, he must find them and warn them that a killer was on the loose.

But first things first. He was on the point of making a dash for one of the blankets beneath the tent and wrapping himself in it when the sound of approaching voices caused him to crouch even lower behind his bush.

He peered out among the leaves, fearing to see four females held at knifepoint. Instead, the total was only two, and they were anything but terrorized.

Indeed, his aunt and the woman who occupied his dreams were chatting as though they had not a care in all the world. Lavinia carried a basket piled high with mushrooms and other mysterious fungi. Catherine had a bundle of some sort cradled in her arms. Jeremy's eyes bulged in their sockets and his jaw tightened as he recognized his clothes.

He was stunned at first by such treachery. And the fact that it had been perpetrated by the two women he valued more than any others on this earth was a blow from which he might not ever recover.

Shock was quickly supplanted by rage. His impulse was to dash into their camp and give the two traitors the tongue-lashing they deserved. But just

148

as he was about to do so, he recalled his natural state. A tongue-lashing by a man appearing à l'Adam, without benefit of that gentleman's dignity-enhancing fig leaf, was bound to lose a great deal of its sting. He might, in fact, merely wind up making a complete cake of himself.

Other voices, coming from a different direction, now assailed his ears. He beat a hasty but noiseless retreat back into the woodland cover. Skulking behind a very expansive tree trunk, he was able to catch glimpses of the four campers as they happily set about making preparations for a meal. Jeremy's soul was filled with bitterness. The sight of the merry foursome was enough, almost, to make him long for the convict's appearance.

He thereupon slunk away into the thickening woods, too furious for sensible thought. But a rumbling from his stomach, which seemed unaware that he was beset with other problems, reminded him that he had more need than ever to keep up his strength. As he changed his course to head toward the berry patch (he was too miserable to note that he was becoming something of a woodsman), *At least*, he thought, *I don't have to worry myself about encountering the so-called ladies*. But he did have to be concerned over whether or not they had emptied the bramble bushes of all their fruit. *It would be the sort of thing they would do*, he fumed. He was only mildly relieved to discover this was not the case. For the thought of perishing here in the wilderness and becoming a black burden on the consciences of Lady Lavinia and Catherine held considerable appeal.

He picked and ate, too engrossed in furious thought to pay proper attention to the havoc that the briars were wreaking on his body. He did emit a snarled curse when a spiky tendril attached itself to his bare bottom. But he quickly picked it off and went on thinking. By the time he had picked the brambles clean, a steely calm had crept over him. He was resolved upon a course of action.

The first order of business was clothing. For nudity, he had decided, was a degrading business. It did nothing for a cove's self-confidence. He immediately set about remedying that situation, taking a page from Adam's book, since he was beginning to feel far more than the usual affinity with man's progenitor.

Fig leaves were, of course, de rigueur for the well-dressed primitive. But these, he suspected, were in short supply, although he would not have known one if he saw it. But he set about collecting the largest species he could find and then mulled over the problem of how to weave the leaves together. Briars were immediately rejected. Effective, but excruciating, like something that would appeal to Christian martyrs, making the hair shirt recreational by contrast. His searching soon turned up some string-size vines with which he was able to lash his leaves together, then tie the fabric around his waist.

The task at last completed, he was inordinately proud of the results. Leaves and vines might not be precisely Bond Street, but they certainly went a long way toward restoring a cove's aplomb. He was only sorry that he did not have a looking-glass. By Jove, he just might preen a bit. Lacking that amenity, there was no more that he could do. He found a mossy spot, well concealed by trees and shrubs, and was soon asleep.

* * *

Catherine, in the meantime, had been almost as conscience-stricken as Jeremy could have wished. It was one thing to teach the impudent young man a lesson. She certainly did not regret dousing him with soapy water when he'd taken liberties with the "upstairs maid." But there were limits. So while Lavinia was engaged in adding new ingredients to her stew pot and then vigorously stirring the questionable results, she bundled up Lord Jeremy's clothing and slipped furtively out of camp.

She returned to the scene of the crime, but caught no glimpse of Jeremy, in or out of the water. Concluding that in his natural state he would be reluctant to make his presence known, she went through an elaborate charade, holding up the clothing for any unseen presence to observe and then placing the bundle underneath the selfsame bush from which it had been taken. Her conscience thus appeased, Catherine hurried back to camp, ready to face her ladyship's displeasure.

Chapter
Twenty-two

THE EVENING PASSED PLEASANTLY ENOUGH FOR THE majority of the campers. Even Jane and Addie were beginning to congratulate themselves upon the way they had adapted to their primitive surroundings. If anyone had told them a few days before that they could survive without servants, let alone all the other amenities of a civilized society, they would have hooted at the notion. But now they were constantly amazed at their resourcefulness. Jane, for instance, perhaps more highly motivated than the others where her meals were concerned, had contrived an ingenious snare made of vines into which an unwary rabbit had wandered to its doom. She had turned a deaf ear to Addie's lament for the poor little thing and had butchered it herself. The skin was now drying on a rock. (It was bound to be useful for something.) Indeed, as Addie had remarked, they were actually beginning to believe that there might, after all, be some point to the Pickering Club. They were certainly not the same helpless females that they had been.

By contrast, the club leader herself was inclined to become more preoccupied as the evening wore on. She put up little resistance when Jane flatly refused to put her rabbit in the pot along with all the questionable examples of nature's bounty that simmered there. "The stew would benefit from a bit of flesh and broth," Lavinia had pointed out.

"The stew would benefit from being dumped," Jane retorted as she devised a spit.

"Nonsense. If you had the slightest concept of good nutrition, you would realize that my stew is far, far better for your health than those multi-course meals you normally stuff yourself with. Just a little of my stew will go a long, long way."

"Well, you'll certainly get no argument with me about that."

The set-down look Lady Lavinia gave her friend was not up to her usual standards. Nor was the compliant way in which she hoisted the heavy stew pot from the fire to make room to roast the rabbit.

For the truth was, she was growing more and more uneasy about her nephew and was having second thoughts regarding the odious trick she had played upon him. She had expected Jeremy, upon discovering that his clothes had been taken, to come creeping up to their camp and, while modestly concealed behind some sheltering shrub, wave a leafy equivalent to the white flag. That he had not done so was making her ladyship increasingly anxious. Perhaps he had come to harm.

At best, her city-bred nephew would be no woodsman, and now, naked and vulnerable—it did not bear thinking on. Still, Jeremy was nothing if not stubborn. He probably wished her to be thinking the way that she was. He was certain to show up soon.

Ah! What was that? Her already-pricked-up ears strained harder. Could it be? Sure enough, there it was again. A faint rustling in those bushes just beyond the light shed by their campfire. Lady Lavinia relaxed.

"Listen!" Addie whispered. Jane stopped turning her rabbit upon its spit while Catherine ceased picking out nut meats with a pin. They both cocked their heads attentively. "There it goes again. There's something out there."

"I am sure it is nothing we should fret about." Lavinia gave Catherine a knowing look, then raised her voice a bit. "It is probably some harmless creature of the night."

"Like a b-bear, you mean?" Addie asked anxiously.

"No. Our harmless creature is more likely of the two-legged variety. Very well, Jeremy," she called, "we know you are there. The game is over. Catherine, fetch his clothing."

In reply, a deadly looking pistol came poking out of an elderberry bush. "Don't nobody move," a deep voice growled.

A high voice screamed.

"Oh, for heaven's sake, Adelaide, do be quiet. It is only Jeremy playing a tasteless prank. Do put that weapon away, Jeremy, before it goes off. As soon as you are decent, you may join us for supper. Catherine, the clothes." She motioned toward the tent.

"I said, don't move."

The bush rustled, then parted, and the pistol, pointed at Lavinia's heart, entered the campfire circle.

It was held by a wild-eyed, desperate-looking creature who almost defied the classification human. He was a huge hulk of a man, intended by nature to be stout but now starved down to the bone. His face blazed with a bright-red stubble; a dirty kerchief concealed any hair on his head that might have matched. He was dressed in a coarse gray shirt and trousers that had been soaked in water, smothered in mud, and snared by briars. His shoes were cracked, the soles flapping. But his most conspicuous article of attire was the great iron fastened on his leg.

The four ladies stared, open-mouthed, at this appendage. It shared his attention. "You there, the screecher." He nodded toward Addie. "Fetch me a file."

Her response was to utter a soft moan and swoon.

"There is no need to terrorize." Lavinia spoke sharply. "Jane, there is a file among the tools the Gypsy left us. You get it for this man. It is in the tent."

"Do like she says," the convict growled, "and don't try anything funny. You there, stay still!" He shifted the pistol's aim in Catherine's direction.

She froze in her tracks. "I only wished to see to Miss Addie," she gulped.

"Never mind, m'dear." Lavinia spoke with her usual crispness. "Adelaide will be all right. She is much better off as she is."

"And you keep your trap closed unless spoke to."

The convict seemed to resent having his authority usurped. "I'm the one as says wot's wot. Wot's keeping the fat one? Hey, you there," he called out, "hurry it up."

"I can't find the file. Where it is, Lavinia?" Jane shouted as she picked it up while wildly looking around for anything that might serve them as a weapon.

"Underneath my blanket," Lavinia called back, and Jane rushed to look there. She could hardly contain her disappointment when instead of the pistol or knife she had hoped to find, there was only a pair of sewing scissors, rather dull at that. "Damn," she muttered as she concealed them in the pocket of her pantaloons.

The convict had collapsed to a sitting position and was leaning back against a tree. There was no doubt that he was in a weakened state. The hand that held the pistol trembled. He solved this problem by resting it upon a knee and aiming it at the still-unconscious Addie. "If one of you so much as thinks of stepping out of line," he snarled, "your friend 'ere gets it.

"Now then, you get busy with that thing," he ordered as Jane approached, gingerly holding the file out toward him. "And you"—he waved the pistol in Catherine's direction—"go sit by the one wot's on the ground there. Closer!" he ordered as Catherine obeyed. "I want to keep the both of you in me sights. And you, old lady"—he nodded toward Lavinia, who bridled at the term—"fetch me wotever that is wot's roasting on your fire."

Lavinia stalked over to the campfire and gave the spit a turn. "The rabbit is not fit to eat," she pronounced. "Thanks to your arrival, it is burnt on one side and raw on the other. I had best give you some of my stew instead. It should still be warm." She moved toward the iron pot and picked up the ladle.

"Stop right there!" the convict barked. "That's clever, that is, lady. But I wasn't born yesterday, you know. And they don't call me the Fox just because Fox 'appens to be me last name. It's that evil brew of yours I've been smelling for the better part of an hour. And the smell alone was enough to do me stomach in. Even the swill they fed us in prison was perfume compared to it. I don't know wot you're stewing there." He directed his gaze toward the rabbit pelt. "Something to remove the 'air from an animal skin is me guess. But I know you didn't intend it for eating. And if you 'opes to poison me with it, you'd best find another 'ope."

"Do not be ridiculous." Lady Lavinia lowered the ladle into the pot. "I made this stew myself and can assure you that its nutritional value is of the highest. It is the very thing to restore—"

"Stop wot you're doing!" The pistol had shifted her way. "Now bring me that rabbit."

"But I just told you. It is not fit—"

"Bring it!" The growl in his throat became feral.

"B-better do as he says, Lavinia." Jane giggled hysterically. "I t-told you nobody would be desperate enough to eat your stew."

"Shut up and file!"

Jane proceeded with her task, her teeth clenched tightly together to stop their chatter, her breath shallow both from fear and from an attempted avoidance of the convict's smell, a condition that made his criticism of the stew's aroma a case of the kettle name-calling the pot. Her fingers were

157

numb, the file was dull, and despite the rapid, rasping noise that acerbated the raw state of her nerves, she made little progress. She wondered distractedly how this would read in the club minutes. *Tuesday, the 9th. Learned to file through a convict's iron.* Lavinia was right. Pickering Club membership did broaden one's horizons.

Lady Lavinia poked the half-charred half-raw rabbit toward the convict on a stick. He snatched it with his free hand and took a voracious bite. "Go sit with them other two," he said thickly, gesturing with the gun.

"Did no one ever tell you not to talk with your mouth full?" she retorted as she complied.

For a time the rasp of the file competed with the sound of the convict eating. Jane had hunted, reluctantly, in her time. The unwelcome vision of dogs tearing into a fox came between her and her task.

" 'Ere, you." The convict's appetite was sated enough for him to notice what she was doing. He was not pleased. "That ain't fingernails you're working on, you know. That there is an iron chain. Put some muscle in it, or you'll get wot for." The pistol flourished Jane's way, and she flinched away from it. She did increase her speed. Its effectiveness proved minimal.

"You there." The convict turned his glare toward Catherine, who had cradled Addie's head upon her lap. "You look young enough to 'ave a bit of strength left in your 'ands. Come 'ere and take over the filing. And you"—the pistol waved toward Jane—"go fetch me a drink of something. Ale for choice."

"Adam's ale is all we have," Lavinia informed

158

him as Catherine shifted Addie carefully and rose. "We are determined to consume only what nature provides."

The convict's snort was eloquent. But he took the dipper from Jane's hand and drank thirstily. He then began to look about him with the pistol now leveled at Catherine's head. The food seemed to be having a salubrious effect. He sat up straighter and craned his neck, taking in his surroundings. "You ladies appear to 'ave done well for yourselves. As soon as I get rid of me chain, I'll see wot I can make good use of. My God, wot's that?"

A rustle in the bushes on the other side of their clearing made him whip his gun that way. "Come out of there, you!" he shouted, while at the same time apparently weighing the probability of hitting a moving target at that range by the light of a flickering campfire. He changed his tactics. The pistol shifted back toward Catherine's head. "One false move and I splatter this little lady's brains from 'ere to Bath."

Chapter
Twenty-three

CATHERINE'S FILE FROZE AGAINST THE CHAIN. Jane's eyes tried to penetrate the darkness while she prayed for a company of militia to be creeping toward them. *Run, Jeremy, run,* Lavinia pleaded silently. *Do not try to be a hero. Go for help.*

The bushes rustled once again.

"I meant wot I said," the convict shouted. Catherine dropped the file and prepared to die.

And then the bushes parted and the Gypsy's horse, roused from sleep by the sound of voices, plodded toward them, trailing his tether behind.

"By gawd, it's an 'orse," the convict cackled. "You ladies 'ave an 'orse. Now I can ride out of 'ere proper like."

"No, you can't." Amazed to be still among the living, Catherine took advantage of the fact with one last deed of kindness. "That animal is ill. He's not nearly strong enough to hold your weight."

"Then if 'e drops, I'll eat 'im," the convict replied practically. "One way or another, me and that animal leaves 'ere together. 'Ere, let's take a look at wot you've done." He inspected the chain and swore. "You're no better than the old 'un. Get back over there with the rest." He gestured with the pistol and Catherine scrambled to obey. "Reckon as 'ow I'll 'ave to file this orf meself. Trust a pack of females to be useless. I'm warning you. I've got me strength back now, and if one of you so much as moves a muscle while I'm filing, I'll blast away at whichever one's the easiest to hit." His eyes dwelled for a bit on Jane.

Addie stirred, moaned softly, and her eyelids fluttered. But to her friends' relief, she lapsed once again into unconsciousness.

Lady Lavinia had enough on her mind without coping with hysteria. Relieved as she had been when the horse, not Jeremy, had emerged into the firelight, she was now almost overcome with dread. She could not even consider their own peril properly for worrying about his. For she alone had been responsible for leaving her dearest kin in a naked, vulnerable state.

Where was he? She resolutely pushed away the thought that the convict might have already killed him. Certainly they would have heard a pistol shot. And Jeremy was young and strong. He boxed, for heaven's sake, with the ex-pugilistic champion of England. He would have been more than a match for a middle-aged, half-starved, desperate—the last adjective undid her.

Suppose Mr. Fox had come sneaking up behind, a large rock in his hand. "Stop it!" Lavinia muttered, causing the convict to pause in his filing and growl

"Be quiet, you." This would not do. She must find a way to get them out of this coil. Lavinia thought furiously while the file rasped.

"That does it!" The convict grunted with satisfaction as his shackles parted. He turned his full attention upon the ladies. "You there. The fat one. Undress."

"I beg your pardon? Were you addressing me, sir?" Jane was at her starchiest.

"That's right, strip."

"Go ahead and fire your pistol, for I shall do no such thing."

"Do not be a fool, Jane," Lavinia snapped. "I collect it is your clothing he wants, and not your body."

"You're right as rain there, ma'am." The convict leered. "If I was up to that kind of start, it'd be the young 'un who'd be peeling for me. Them ridiculous-looking outfits ain't wot I'd pick if given me choice, but it's better that I'm mistook for a fugitive from the circus than from the jail. Now, hurry it up, old girl. If it's modesty you're worried about, you can have me own uniform."

Jane, turning pale at the thought of his filthy, lice-infested garments, stood and slowly began to remove her tunic, blessing Lavinia for the thoroughness that had moved her to design a short chemise and cotton underdrawers to go with her pageboy creation. Even so, her cheeks were bricky red as she tossed her outer garments toward the convict. The scissors fell out at his feet. He picked them up and felt their point. "Planning to cut hot butter, was you?" he mocked, but pocketed them all the same. Jane and Catherine modestly averted their gazes while he changed his clothes. Lavinia used the moment of his inattention to ease closer to the fire.

The desperado was certainly transformed. Into what was difficult to say. The tunic strained tightly across his shoulders, too small for him to button the placket in the back. And the ankle-length pantaloons made it only to his shins. Still, there was no doubt it was an improvement over his prison garb. " 'Ere." He threw his discarded garments at Jane's feet and laughed as she recoiled from them. "Suit yerself," he chuckled. "You can travel in your drawers, for all of me." But then he paused and frowned. "No, that won't do. Likely to make folk wonder a bit too much. So unless you've got a change of clothes in your tent there, I reckon as 'ow you'll 'ave to put on mine. We'll all be queer-looking enough without you shocking the country folk."

"What do you mean 'we'?" Lavinia frowned.

"Just that you ladies are going to help me escape." The convict grinned evilly. "Nobody's going to expect me to be part of a Gypsy band, or wotever it is you types are got up as."

Before her friends had time to react to this announcement, Addie moaned again, then sat up abruptly. "Where am I?" Still dazed, she looked vaguely around her.

"It is all right, Adelaide," Lavinia said. "It is all right. We are here."

"Where's here?" Addie's eyes then lighted on the convict. "Oh, my!" She reached out and clutched at Jane, who patted her hand comfortingly. "There, there. It's all right," she murmured.

"Why is he wearing your clothes?" Addie whispered.

"He wishes to be a Pickering."

"Oh."

Addie stared once more at the convict, who, dissatisfied with the length of his sleeves, was rolling them up above his elbows. "It fits him remarkably well, doesn't it?"

"It does not! It is miles too small," Jane began indignantly. But she was cut short by the look of horror that had suddenly suffused her friend's face.

Addie screamed.

All three ladies wheeled toward the convict, expecting him to be on the point of murdering them then and there. But Mr. Fox, who knew better, followed the direction of Addie's gaze and spun around just as Jeremy came leaping from the bushes, a wild-looking figure, fierce, filthy, scratched, unshaven, leaf-kilted, and brandishing a club.

The plan, formed in a few minutes wait in the bushes while he surveyed the scene, had been to sneak up on the convict from the rear and cosh him unawares. Addie's scream had changed all that. The convict managed to grab Jeremy's wrist as he tried to swing his club. They were immediately locked in mortal combat, straining this way and that, emitting blood-curdling growls and oaths, each trying to wrestle the other to the ground.

Lavinia leapt into action. She heaved up the iron pot, the only weapon she could find at hand, and joined the fray, whooping encouragement to her nephew while she looked for an opportunity to swing her makeshift mace. The problem was that every time she had a clear shot at the convict's head, the combatants shifted ground. After she had come within a hairbreadth of braining Jeremy, she realized that the situation called for different tactics. Ever resourceful, Lady Lavinia flung the contents of the pot over both combatants.

There were simultaneous howls of anguish as the

two men sprang apart, gasping and swiping at their eyes. "Dear God, I'm blind!" Jeremy croaked. The convict hadn't time to utter. His head, now an open target, caught the full impact of the cast-iron pot. He went down like a felled oak with a reverberant thud.

"Ladies, turn your backs!"

Lady Lavinia, now in full command of the situation, was quick to discover that her nephew's loincloth had not survived the struggle in anything resembling its original state. Indeed, the ground around him looked like an early fall, so liberally was it strewn with leaves. "Are you all right, Jeremy?" she asked anxiously.

"Oh, yes. Certainly. Of course. Indeed." He spoke with heavy sarcasm. He had managed to clear his eyes enough to see, but their expression was baleful as he glared at his revered aunt. "It wasn't enough, I collect, that you left me naked and starving. You had to blind and humiliate me as well. Not even to mention leaving me smelling worse than any self-respecting skunk. What is this noxious mess, anyhow?" His nose wrinkled with disgust.

The convict stirred and moaned.

"Never mind that now. Let's get this fellow tied up before he comes to. Jane," she called, "fetch us that leftover tent rope.

"Now then, Jeremy," she ordered after Jane, carefully averting her eyes, had handed her the rope, "help me drag him over to that tree and secure him against it."

"Oh, surely you don't require my assistance." The sentence was awash with bitterness. "I am sure you can manage best on your own."

"Now, my dear boy, there is no need to take that tone." Together they were dragging the convict back to his old position. "What sort of person would I be if I stood idly by and did not try to aid my own flesh and blood?"

"The kind of person who has faith in her own flesh and blood's ability to protect you, that's who."

They propped the limp Mr. Fox against the tree trunk. Lavinia started to secure him there, then changed her mind and handed the rope to Jeremy. He accepted it sullenly and soon had lashed the convict like Ulysses to the mast. "I am sure you are longing to check the knots. Pray don't let consideration of my pride stop you. It is already tramped to a pulp."

"Really, Jeremy, you are behaving like a two-year-old. You acted very heroically. And if Addie had not screeched in that fashion and alerted Mr. Fox, you would have finished him off with admirable dispatch."

The other ladies, still with their backs turned, had missed none of the dialogue.

"I'm s-so sorry," Addie now blubbered. "But how was I to know? You looked not at all like yourself, dear Jeremy. I th-thought you were a wild man from Borneo."

"That is quite understandable."

"C-can you ever forgive me?"

"*You* have no need to be forgiven," he said pointedly.

Catherine stole a glance back over her shoulder. And once assured she had not turned into a pillar of salt, she quickly removed her pantaloons and flung them in Jeremy's direction. "Put these on. You'll feel much better."

"You think so?" He picked up the garment and eyed it askance. "I doubt it will fit."

"Well, pray don't point out that I am the largest here," Jane threw in bitterly. "Mr. Fox there is wearing my ensemble."

"Let me suggest, Jeremy"—by her own standards, Lavinia spoke diffidently—"that you bathe in the stream first, then don your own clothing. Catherine's is a needless sacrifice. Your things are in the tent."

"They are?" Jane was incredulous. "You mean there was male attire on hand and you let that odious villain take my clothes?"

"Now, don't you climb up into the boughs, too, Jane." Lavinia's patience was becoming strained. "I knew Jeremy's need was greater than yours. Your shift and drawers cover you quite adequately."

"Then suppose you give me your costume and let's see just how adequate you find your shift and drawers."

"Ladies, please. Will someone just point me toward my clothes?"

"Catherine dear, would you please fetch them for him. There are in my portmanteau."

"No, I'm afraid they aren't there any longer." Catherine looked and sounded quite contrite.

"Don't tell me. You cut my things up into strips and braided a hearth rug."

"Nothing of the kind. I just had second thoughts, that's all. I'm sorry, Lady Lavinia, but it did rather seem like an odious trick, so I took Lord Jeremy's clothing back where we had found them."

"Did you now?" For the first time there was a slight thaw in Jeremy's voice.

"I can go fetch them."

"Not till daylight," Lavinia said firmly. "In the meantime Jeremy can wrap himself in a blanket. After ridding himself of our stew first, naturally."

Chapter
Twenty-four

A T FIRST LIGHT CATHERINE GUIDED JEREMY BACK TO
the stream bank. He was clad in Addie's Nor-
wich shawl which he wore kilt-fashion, a style he
had grown so accustomed to, he observed, that he
might never go back to more conventional, restric-
tive attire. Nonetheless, he fairly pounced upon his
garments with an "Ah-ha!" of joy. "This does rather
seem a pointless concession to convention," he said
dryly moments later as he stepped behind a bush
to put them on. "It seems I have no secrets from
you."

"I have seen quite a lot of you lately, that's true."
Catherine did not quite manage to smother her giggle.

"Oh, go ahead and laugh." He emerged from the
bushes, tattered, dirty, but clothed. "I'm painfully
aware that I have cut a ridiculous figure."

"Oh, I would not say that." She colored a bit. "I thought you looked rather like one of the better Elgin marbles."

"A Greek god slathered in green slime? Now, there's a picture for you.

"But anyhow, I do thank you for having a change of heart and at least trying to restore my clothing. It's comforting to know that you are not wholly indifferent to my well-being." He was moving toward her, a determined look in his eye that should have been alarming. Perhaps it was and Catherine was simply too intimidated to retreat. Or perhaps being in his arms had become habit-forming. For whatever reason, she found herself being kissed with the primal ardor of one who had recently been stripped of all conventions and was giving full reign to the natural man.

It was instinctive on her part at first to play a willing Eve to Jeremy's Adam. The brook, the trees, the warbling birds, all conspired to lend a sense of paradise. But a proper young lady's breeding is bound, eventually, to out. Therefore, after a lengthy, blissful interval, Catherine regained her senses and extracted herself. "Oh, I am so sorry," she gasped. "I should not have behaved so."

"Of course you should have." He reached for her once more. "That's what people in love do. Behave so, that is. It has been a given all along that I love you. Am I wrong to suspect the feeling is mutual?"

This time she pushed him away with real determination. "No. You don't understand. What I may or may not feel for you is beside the point. You know nothing at all about me, you see."

He looked down tenderly into her tormented face.

"I have been hoping for ages that you would remedy that situation."

"And I was hoping that I would not need to." She took a shuddering breath. "Now it seems I have no choice. I am sorry, Lord Jeremy, for what has passed between us. I should never have allowed myself to go so far. You see, I am married."

"Fustian!"

"No, it's true."

"It is true that you spoke your vows. But unless I much mistake the matter, it, ah, takes a bit of, er, physical cooperation between the bride and groom before they are considered truly wed."

"You knew?" She stared in disbelief. Disbelief rapidly turned to indignation. "Why did you not say something?"

"Why did I not say something? I kept waiting for you to trust me, not even to mention trusting those intrepid members of the Pickering Club who have taken you to their bosoms—albeit in Aunt Addie's case a false one. I hoped you'd confide in me of your own free will. But now I can't afford to wait for that. Monkhouse is in Bath, you see. That's why I came looking for you."

"Oh, dear God." She went as pale as death, and this time he did pull her into his arms.

"Don't worry. He won't come combing Bathwick Wood for you. And in the meantime we will decide what to do for the best. I say"—he broke off suddenly—"do you hear something?"

He had been vaguely conscious of a baying sound far in the distance. It was now growing clearer and frantic.

"Hounds! Come on!" He grasped Catherine by the hand and raced with her toward the camp.

They arrived in a dead heat with the dogs who broke out of the woods to encircle the tethered convict. The frenzied yapping mingled with Addie's screams to guide the lawmen who were following the hounds straight to the fugitive. They rushed up to Mr. Fox with triumphant whoops, then as quickly backed away from his pungent odor.

Mr. Fox appeared relieved to see them. "After all the 'ell I've been through at the 'ands of these bedlamite females," he informed them, "the hulks will seem restful."

The law officers, having first doused their prisoner with several kettles of water from the brook, then sat down to drink the tea Lavinia provided. Jeremy took advantage of the lull to draw the Pickerings aside.

"I think we need to powwow," he whispered. "That is the appropriate term, is it not? You can't stay in this wood any longer, ladies. For when these officers get back to town, they are certain to tell all and sundry about the peculiar—distinctive—group of ladies who captured their escapee for them. The tale will spread like wildfire. It will become the *on-dit* of the Pump Room. And Lord Monkhouse is presently visiting in Bath."

"Do you mean Colonel Marston's nephew?" Addie asked. "But why should that matter?"

"I think you had best tell them, Catherine."

And, after a moment's hesitation, Catherine poured out the story of her forced marriage and subsequent flight.

Addie was all tearful sympathy. Jane was hotly indignant. Lavinia, who, after all, had been ninety nine percent certain of her charge's history, was frowning thoughtfully. "Have you no relations,

Catherine, other than the witless aunt and uncle who forced you into such an unsuitable liaison?"

"My mother's brother, Sir Jonathan Fowler, is in the diplomatic corps. Right after you employed me, I wrote to the latest address I had for him, in Brussels, to tell him of my plight. But he has always moved about a great deal and I fear my letter has not reached him. At least I've had no word."

"Of course he would expect you to still be in London," Lady Lavinia mused. "We shall have to see if there has been any reply there. But if not, never mind. I know the archbishop personally and shall approach him about procuring an annulment. I had thought it might add weight to our case to have some member of your family present. But if that proves impossible, I shall act in loco parentis. The archbishop will not refuse my request."

No one doubted that for a moment.

"Now then. As Jeremy has pointed out, we should not remain here. It is best not to risk a confrontation with Lord Monkhouse, though I must confess I quite long to give that young man a piece of my mind. I think Bristol will be safe now, since Monkhouse has already searched there for Catherine. Do you not agree?" She did not wait for acquiescence but went on formulating her plans aloud. "Jeremy, you will return to Bath immediately and see to it that our things are packed."

"Does that mean that you do not intend to let the Bristol folk see those fetching costumes?" His lips twitched.

"A man so recently clothed in leaves—and by the bye, I compliment you on your resourcefulness—has no business casting aspersions on anyone else's departure from convention. And what is more, even

Jane will agree that our uniforms are most suitable and liberating."

"I will agree that I much prefer them over my present chemise and drawers."

"But we stray from the issue at hand. While you are in Bath, Jeremy, send a footman to London to see if there is any message from Catherine's uncle. And we should leave word there of our Bristol direction. But impress upon the servants the need for secrecy. Promise a lavish tip if they hold their tongues."

The best Jeremy could manage under his aunt's frowning chaperonage was to take Catherine's hand and implore her not to worry. "All will be right and tight, you'll see." Then he was off, leading, at Lavinia's instruction, the Gypsy horse to present to the farmer who was stabling his equipage.

"Do you think he will consider this bag of bones worth its oats?" Jeremy looked at the beast dubiously.

"Of course. The creature has greatly improved in the short time we have had him. And with a little care he should turn into a quite useful farm animal."

The law officers, too, were preparing to depart with their fugitive. Addie crept into the tent while no one was noticing and tore a page from the pristine Pickering Club notebook which Lavinia had insisted that each member bring. She quickly scribbled a note and slipped it, along with several coins, to the least fearsome-looking minion of the law.

The note was delivered to Colonel Marston's rooms just as two burly men, whose battered faces and misshapen ears marked them as pugilists, were leaving. Their expressions reflected satisfaction. The colonel's face was set and grim. It brightened immediately, however, upon deciphering Mrs. Oliver's hastily scrawled message.

"Wallace, pack me things!" he shouted. "I'm off to Bristol."

The colonel was in his dressing room being shaved when his nephew arrived a few minutes later. He glared at the young man's reflection in the glass. "No time to talk now, Hugh. Been called out of town on urgent business. But we will have a heart-to-heart when I return. Of that you can be sure. Now, begone, sir."

On his way out, Lord Monkhouse paused in the bedchamber to reflect upon his uncle's odd behavior and help himself to a glass of claret. The colonel's purse and spectacles, along with an unfolded piece of paper, were lying on the bedside table next to the crystal decanter. Monkhouse glanced at the note absently, then snatched it up. His eyes narrowed as he read. He carefully replaced the note where he had found it and strode across the room. He broke his stride at the doorway, however, to pause a moment and shrug. He then returned to the bedside table and helped himself to several bank notes from the purse that was lying there.

Chapter
Twenty-five

*L*ADY LAVINIA WAS ON THE POINT OF MAKING THEIR arrangements with the innkeeper when her nephew, with a frown, preempted her. Giving the name John Morrison, he secured three bedchambers and a private parlor for an indefinite period. Jeremy had succeeded in getting Catherine's uncle's latest address from the foreign office. Lady Lavinia had sent an urgent message by courier. The plan was to remain in Bristol until they heard from him.

With uncharacteristic meekness Lavinia fell in with Jeremy's suggestion that she and Catherine share a room while Adelaide and Jane take the other. She did, however, strongly object to Jeremy's occupying the bedchamber next to her and Catherine. "The rooms even have a contacting door." She took him aside to point this out reprovingly.

"I know. I made sure of it, in fact."

His aunt's frown deepened. "I am aware, Jeremy, of your feelings for Catherine. But it should not be necessary to point out that until her marriage is dissolved, there should be no grounds for scandal. You yourself told me that the gossip-mongers were already saying there must be another man involved. I do not want the archbishop to think that there is any other motive besides Lord Monkhouse's reprehensible character to account for Catherine's flight. We will avoid all appearance of impropriety."

"What we will do is avoid any possibility of Monk's getting to Catherine before we can have the marriage annulled. I am far better acquainted with that swine's 'reprehensible character' than you are, and I will take no chances with her safety. Besides, can anyone seriously think I would invade a bed-chamber that you guarded like a dragon? You give me too much credit, ma'am."

"I am not certain that I care for your choice of words, nephew."

"Dragon I said, and dragon I stick by."

In spite of these apprehensions, they were a merry group as they shared a supper in their parlor. "Clean, proper gowns and all of this," Jane chortled as the waiters arrived with heaping platters of lamb, veal, turkey, and assorted vegetables. "Thanks to your stew, Lavinia, I shall never take good food for granted again."

"You have never taken food for granted, Jane," her friend riposted. "You have always eaten as though someone were waiting to snatch away your plate."

The ladies decided upon an early night, the prospects of genuine feather beds proving an irresistible lure. Jeremy, however, opted to visit the public room before retiring, ostensibly for a nightcap but in reality to see if any other travelers might have arrived from Bath.

The ladies said their good-nights in the corridor before retiring to their adjoining rooms. Lavinia's first act upon entering their chamber was to turn the keys in both connecting doors. When Catherine gave her an odd look, the reason she voiced was that Addie was prone to sleepwalk, especially when under strain. "I do not wish to find her standing over our bed in the wee hours of the night like a specter from some lurid Gothic novel."

After she and Catherine had changed into their nightclothes, Lavinia carried their traveling dresses over to the huge clothes press that took up a large portion of the wall they shared with Jane and Addie. As she opened the press door, she was looking back over her shoulder to address a remark. So it was Catherine's terror-stricken expression that first alerted her to the danger. By the time she turned her head, a pistol was already pressed against it, her upper arm was held in a viselike grip, and she found herself staring into the bloodshot eyes of Lord Monkhouse.

"If either of you makes a sound," he whispered as he stepped down from the press, "I'll put a bullet through this old harridan's skull."

"You will do no such thing," Lavinia said levelly, "for the report would bring everyone in the inn here immediately. Go ahead and scream, Catherine."

"Do and I'll kill her. I'm a desperate man, I warn you." And as though to prove his point, he drew back his arm and aimed a savage blow with the pistol butt at Lady Lavinia's temple. She sank limply to the floor.

"Not a sound or I'll finish her." Monkhouse carefully detached the bellpull from the wall and secured her ladyship's hands behind her. He reached inside the dark coat he wore and pulled out a handkerchief. With hands that trembled slightly he tied this around her face.

"You'll smother her—unless she's dead already." Catherine's voice to her own ears seemed to come from miles away. She had been in the act of preparing for bed and now stood barefoot in her shift, frozen with fear.

Monkhouse lifted Lavinia's limp body and stuffed it in the press, closing the door. He then turned the pistol toward Catherine. "Now then, Lady Monkhouse," he said softly, "you've led me a merry chase, but we are finally going to have the honeymoon you ran from."

"Lady Lavinia is right, you know." Catherine backed away from him. "Fire that pistol and help will come."

"But it will be a bit late for you, won't it, my dear? And don't think I am bluffing. For unless we are wed, properly, I am a dead man anyhow. Oh, there's no need to look so horrified, m'lady. You aren't being ravished, you know. It is not as though we haven't had all the holy mumbo-jumbo said over us. If all else fails, you can always close your eyes and think of Pickering." He started toward her just as a frantic thumping began in the clothes press.

"What is that?"

Addie, who had been on the point of falling asleep, sat upright in bed.

"Oh, for heaven's sake," Jane complained as the wall behind her reverberated. "What a time for Lavinia to be pounding."

"They must have bugs." Addie shuddered at the thought as Jane, too, sat up in bed and thumped back at the wall. "Be quiet in there," she shouted. "Some of us would like to get some sleep."

In reply, the thumping increased to a veritable drumroll.

Uttering a most unladylike single syllable, Jane dashed out of bed and started for the connecting door.

"What are you doing?"

"I am going to see whether or not Lavinia has lost her mind. And in either case, I plan to give her a piece of mine." She tried to open the door and found it locked. "Lavinia!" She rattled the handle. "Open up!"

Inside the bedchamber, Monkhouse, gun in hand, paused in indecision, looking first at the rocking clothes press and then at the rattling door. "Oh, what the devil," he muttered. "This will take only a moment, and then what's done can't be undone." He lunged for Catherine, who dodged his grasp and screamed.

"Addie, go for help!" Jane shouted as she continued her ineffectual assault upon the door. "Jeremy's downstairs. Hurry, for God's sake. Catherine! Lavinia!" she screamed through the heavy door panel. "Help is coming! Oh, dear God, what is happening in there?"

What was happening was that Catherine was doing her best to elude Monkhouse's grasp as she dodged him about the room. His lordship's liberal consumption of brandy for Dutch courage aided her endeavors for a while, but he eventually managed to corner her, then fling her upon the bed.

Addie had not hesitated at Jane's command. She had gone streaking down the inn corridor unmindful of the figure that she cut with her nightcap dangling by its ribbons around her neck and the skirt of her nightdress hiked up to free her limbs for speed. Nor did she noticed the masculine head that protruded turtle-fashion from a partially open door. Colonel Marston recognized her, however, and followed on her heels. They met Lord Jeremy coming up the stairs.

"Come quick," Addie gasped. "All their doors are locked and something terrible is happening." Without pausing for more details, Jeremy sped past her.

She and the colonel were right behind him when he kicked in the corridor door. And by the time he had shot across the room to snatch Monkhouse by the collar, jerk him away from Catherine, and land a cracking right to his jaw, Lavinia had emerged, untied and ungagged, from the clothes press.

"Shut what remains of that door," she ordered Jane as she joined the group. "We do not wish to have every resident of the inn gawking at us."

Lord Jeremy was too concerned with Catherine to have eyes for anything else. "Are you all right?" His voice was shaky. "Did that bastard—?"

All Catherine could manage was a shake of the head as she reached for her dressing gown to cover her torn shift.

"Jeremy!" Lavinia's shouted warning was too late. Monkhouse had recovered sufficiently to retrieve his pistol from where it lay concealed beneath the bed hangings. He now leveled it at Jeremy's back. "Get out of here, all of you," he croaked, "or I'll blow Gallahad here to hell." His eyes looked glazed, and he swayed a bit as he stood there in his stocking feet with his fine cambric shirt unbuttoned. But not one of them doubted his ability to do just what he said. "No one has the right to interfere with a lawfully wedded husband and his wife. How does it go, m'dear?" He laughed mockingly at Catherine, whose blood had drained from her stark face. "Whom God has joined together let no man put asunder?"

"Leave the almighty out of this, you limb of Satan!" Colonel Marston roared. He took a threatening step toward his nephew, but was halted by the swing of the pistol in his direction and Addie's clutch upon his coattails. Neither act silenced him, however. "Yours was an unholy alliance from the beginning, and I shall testify to both the church and the civil authorities that you married this innocent young woman for the sole purpose of securing her fortune to save yourself from the unscrupulous moneylenders who threatened your life. And to think I actually paid them off," he ranted. "I should have allowed them to tear you limb from limb, as they threatened to do. And I would have, by God, had I realized that anyone of my own blood could behave so knavishly. You have blackened the family name past all repair, Hugh. So go ahead. Shoot me. I can never hold up my head again, in any case. Jeremy my boy, when he fires the barker, jump him." And he took three slow, determined steps toward Lord Monkhouse, tugging Addie, whose fingers had frozen upon his coattails, behind him.

"Adelaide!" Jane tried to jerk her friend away while Lavinia took advantage of the distraction to scoop the ink pot off the writing desk beside her and conceal it behind her back.

"Stop where you are, uncle," Monkhouse ordered. "It's not you I'll shoot, but Pickering. Only first, pray repeat what you just said. You paid my gambling debts?"

"Yes, for my sins." He had halted at the threat. "But let me tell you now, sir, that it is the last penny you will ever get from me. I plan to cut you off."

While Monkhouse's attention was riveted upon his uncle, two things happened: Jeremy sprang for his throat and Lavinia hurled her ink pot. Both missiles were on target.

"God, I've been blinded!"

The shout came from the men struggling on the floor. Unfortunately, it was Jeremy who shouted.

Other occupants of the room had also been galvanized into action. Catherine grabbed the pistol which had been wrestled from Monk's hand. Colonel Marston sprang for the heavy candlestick upon the night table and danced around the writhing, turning combatants till his nephew's head was uppermost. He then crashed his brass cudgel effectively upon target.

"Famous! Oh, how heroic!" Addie crowed, giving the colonel the sort of look that Hector and Hercules were probably accustomed to. The colonel was not. He colored with pleasure.

"You can release Lord Monkhouse, Jeremy," Lavinia said kindly. "He is quite hors de combat."

"You've blinded me. Again, aunt." Lord Jeremy spoke with resigned fatalism as he staggered to his feet.

The villain stirred and moaned and attempted to

sit up. Jane pushed him back down and sat on him. "Someone please fetch a rope," she requested.

Lavinia was too engaged in leading her nephew to the washstand to comply. She filled the basin from the water pitcher there and plunged his face into it.

"That's right, drown me, too," he sputtered as he finally struggled up for air.

"There now, is that better?" She handed him a towel. It turned instantly dark blue, the same cast as his complexion. "Can you see?"

"Yes. Unfortunately." His eyes were focused upon the looking-glass.

"Never mind, dear," his aunt said soothingly. "The color will soon fade. After all, the ancient Britons rather fancied the look. It is not at all unbecoming."

Addie had found the bellpull in the clothes press and had handed it, worshipfully, to the colonel.

"You don't have to do that, you know," Monkhouse said as his uncle began to truss him. "Now that you have been so kind as to discharge my debts and save me from having both legs broken—then worse"—he paused to shudder—"I have no further interest in this woman." He gave Catherine a contemptuous look. "The last thing I ever wanted was to be leg-shackled. So you have a choice, uncle. Turn me over to the authorities and cause a scandal, or let me leave quietly and you'll not hear from me again."

"You'll pay for what you've done, sir," the colonel said between his teeth as he knotted the rope viciously on Monkhouse's wrists.

"Just a moment, Colonel Marston." Lavinia walked over and stared down at the prisoner. Even a nightcap and nightgown could not diminish her noble air. "Do we have your word then that you will not try to interfere in any way with a marriage annulment?"

"You have my assurance, ma'am," the other sneered, "that there is nothing I would like better."

"Then let him go, Colonel. We will all be the worse for any notoriety. I should especially hate to see your distinguished name blackened because of this one blot upon the family escutcheon."

There was a complete silence as Lord Monkhouse left the room. Despite the fact that it was swelling rapidly, his lip had managed to curl in a sneer, and the look that swept the company was contemptuous. Even so, the image of a whipped cur leapt to all their minds.

"Well now!" Lavinia spoke briskly after the battered door had shut behind him. "I think it time that we all get some rest. If you gentlemen will help me push this press in front of the door, Catherine and I should now sleep securely."

This accomplished, Colonel Marston bade them an awkward good-night. He tried to stammer an apology for his nephew's despicable behavior, but Lady Lavinia cut him short. "There is no need for you to upset yourself, sir. You are in no way to blame for your nephew's action. Furthermore, the coincidence of your presence here"—she gave Addie an ironic glance—"has resolved a potentially tragic situation. We are in your debt, sir."

A restored, revitalized Colonel Marston pulled himself up to full military height, clicked his heels in Prussian fashion, bowed in general to the company, and walked almost jauntily toward the adjoining door. Since it connected with her temporary bedchamber, Addie felt a hostess's duty to guide him through it. He paused at the door to the corridor to bend over her hand. His eyes were eloquent. Her face flamed red, whether from pleasure or from a sudden recollection of her dishabille was not really clear.

"I need to speak to you privately," Jane was saying to Lavinia.

"Now?" Her friend stared in disbelief.

"Yes, now." Jane gave her friend a push toward the other bedchamber while Jeremy gave her a grateful look.

When the door had closed behind the ladies, he turned toward Catherine, who was still standing near the bed, clutching the pistol in her hand. "I think you can put that down now," he said gently, and watched while she did so. "Are you all right?"

"Oh, yes. Certainly." She gave a shaky smile. "Indeed, I collect that if I ever cease trembling, I shall be absolutely top of the trees."

"Then perhaps this will help." He swiftly crossed the space between them and took her tenderly in his arms. The prolonged kiss was clearly therapeutic. At its conclusion Catherine looked up at him adoringly, laughed involuntarily, then coughed to cover her gaffe.

"Oh, blast it, I forgot. I'm blue. Remind me to murder my aunt Lavinia."

"It's quite all right. One soon gets used to it. It's rather becoming actually, complements your eyes."

"Oh, do be quiet."

He silenced her effectively. This time the kiss might have broken some sort of duration record if an imperious throat-clearing at the door had not caused the young couple to spring guiltily apart.

Epilogue

"THE MEETING OF THE PICKERING CLUB WILL NOW come to order."

In Grosvenor Square, London, Lady Lavinia emphatically banged her brand-new gavel to the detriment of the library table's mahogany finish. Her two closest friends reluctantly set aside their teacups and wiped the crumbs of seed cake from their bosoms.

The minutes of the last meeting and the treasurer's report were quickly disposed of, since Jane had not bothered to record the former, and as for the latter, the club was devoid of funds.

"Well, never mind," the president brushed aside such trifles with uncharacteristic charity. "No one can possibly say that our first scientific expedition was not an unqualified success." She gave Jane a challenging look. Her friend refused to meet her eyes.

"Very well, then. Our next order of business is the wedding, which, as you know, will take place in Brussels in two months time."

It had not been easy to persuade the impatient young couple to wait, but Lady Lavinia, with the backing of Catherine's uncle, who had arrived in Bristol the day after Lord Monkhouse's rout, had insisted upon an interval long enough to allow the gossip to die down a bit. The pair had also agreed that a marriage abroad, followed by an extended honeymoon tour of Europe, would be wise. Besides, a foreign city should offer new scope for the Pickering Club.

"I have booked our passage," Lavinia informed them, "and am now in the process of designing a shipboard uniform for us. Something with a nautical flair."

The membership groaned in unison.

"And, Adelaide, pray inform Colonel Marston that Catherine is most desirous of having him attend the nuptials. Since he has, coincidentally, already obtained a berth on the same ship and at the same time as we have done"—she looked accusingly at her cousin, who tried to play innocent—"it would be a pity for him not to be present at the ceremony.

"Now then. There remains the matter of the wedding gift. I am, of course, giving the young couple a grand tour for my personal present. But I feel something from the club would be appropriate since Catherine is an associate charter member."

There followed a lively discussion. Such banal suggestions as crystal candlesticks or monogrammed fish slices were scornfully dismissed. "Come, ladies.

We need to think of something that will be reminiscent of the Pickerings."

"Well, Jeremy might appreciate a formula for ink removal," Jane offered.

"Nonsense. He faded long ago."

"I expect that Catherine's natural hair color should also be restored in time for the wedding," Addie mused.

The gavel crashed. "Ladies! Could we please return to the business upon the table!"

It was finally decided that the young couple would be presented with a silver loving cup engraved with the club's coat of arms which Lavinia thereupon volunteered to design. It should, she declared, incorporate the elements of their first adventure.

After considerable controversy, the Pickerings finally agreed upon the following list:

> an iron stew pot
> a starving horse, rampant
> a convict's shackles
> a snared rabbit (Jane's insistence)
> a leafy kilt

This symbolic assortment might have daunted the average practitioner of heraldry. But Lady Lavinia declared herself more than equal to the task.